The Irish Lottery

SIENNA BLAKE

Copyright © 2019 Sienna Blake
First Edition: June 2019
Copyright 2019 Sienna Blake
All rights reserved.

ISBN: 9781072292203

Cover art copyright 2019 Giorgia Foroncelli: giorgiaforoncelli@libero.it. All
Rights Reserved Sienna Blake. Stock images: shutterstock
Content editing services by Book Detailing.
Proofreading services by Proof Positive: http://proofpositivepro.com.

The characters and events portrayed in this book are fictional. Any similarity
to real persons, living or dead, is coincidental and not intended by the author.

For women everywhere.
#YesToYou

Noah

"They said no."

Aubrey Campbell, my very best friend in the whole world, stared back at me, her dark-chocolate eyes misting up with tears as her heart broke for me. "I'm so sorry, Noah."

The bank said no.

My three brothers—Michael, Darren and Eoin—went in together as co-borrowers, pooling our combined incomes. We offered up our family home and I put up my bar, The Jar, for collateral as well.

And they still said no.

I wanted to kick something. To punch something. In fact, I just came from Gallagher's Gym where I spent an hour pounding the crap out of a bag before I came to Aubrey's apartment. Didn't help much. I still wanted to murder someone.

"Where the hell am I going to get a quarter of a million euros?" I ran my hands through my sandy hair. It was still damp from my shower and I was sure it was sticking up everywhere. That was the least of my worries right now. "She needs that surgery, Rey. If she doesn't get it—" I cut off, my throat closing around the consequences. I couldn't even say it. I couldn't even *think* it or I'd lose my shit.

The Irish public health system was…well, it was pretty poor. My ma didn't have health insurance so they'd put her on the public hospital waiting list. It was almost two fucking years long. Our ma needed this surgery. *Now.*

My heart twisted in my chest and I let out a groan.

"It's going to be okay, Noah." Aubrey slipped her slender arms around my waist. "We'll think of something."

We. She said *we.* For a few precious moments, I didn't feel alone.

I wrapped my arms around her, crushing her flush against me. She didn't protest, in fact her arms tightened around my waist.

I rested my chin on her head. Her long dark hair smelled like…tropical beaches, coconuts and pineapple. It must be her shampoo.

Hope was a tiny flame in the heart of this beautiful girl. I never wanted to let her go.

Fuck. I was so in love with my best friend.

But she was engaged to someone else.

Aubrey

Noah stayed for another hour and we just sat on the couch holding each other for most of it. I could tell that he didn't want to talk. He left in a daze, saying he had to get to the bar and he'd call me later. I guess he forgot I'm working tonight, a last-minute swap he begged me to do just this morning.

For the four years I've known Noah O'Sullivan, I've never seen him like this. He's been moody and distant since his mother was diagnosed with a heart condition two weeks ago.

There seemed to be a special kind of relationship between an Irish boy and his mammy. Even more so between the O'Sullivan brothers and theirs as their father has been out of the picture since Eoin, the youngest, was born.

All the O'Sullivan boys were old enough to live away from home but they always went to their ma's place for Sunday lunch. Always.

If their ma passed away—

Oh, God, I couldn't even *think* it. My heart broke for Noah and his brothers.

Even as I got ready for work later that evening, it was all I could think about. I almost put on my work shirt inside out. And shoved my feet into mismatched socks before hiding the error in my fur-lined boots.

A key jangled in the lock as I was grabbing my coat and bag.

Sean walked in, brushing the drops of rain off his dapper grey coat. My fiancé. Baby-faced and clean shaven, his clear blue eyes were startling in his pale skin.

Sean didn't live with me. I lived with a housemate in a two-bedroom flat in the southside of Dublin. But Sean did have a spare key that I gave him once we were engaged. It was my compromise over moving in with him right away. I wanted to wait until we were married to do anything as serious as that. I'd never admit it to anyone, not even Noah, but sometimes at night when I was alone, I'd have something close to a panic attack over the idea of getting married. I mean, I was only twenty-three.

Sean spotted me and paused with the door half open, a chill already wafting in from the foyer. The insulation in these old buildings was horrible. "Where are you going?" he asked.

Ah, shit. I totally forgot that Sean was coming over this evening. "Crap, sorry babe, I told Noah I'd work tonight. One of the girls called in sick this morning."

Sean's shoulders sagged. "You didn't think to tell me?"

"Sorry, it slipped my mind."

His eyes went past me to the mess of screen printing all over the living room. I was glad my housemate was always at her boyfriend's place and rarely home. Even if she was, she was cool with my mess because I always cleaned it up. Eventually. It was my thing. My hobby. It helped take my mind off things. Obviously, it took my mind off things just a little too well.

"Let me guess," Sean said, his mouth set in a line of disapproval. "You were screen printing all afternoon and forgot to tell me."

"Not *all* afternoon."

"Did you send out those resumes like you said you would?"

Shit. "I ran out of time."

"Aubrey!"

"What? I had more important things to do."

"Like what?"

"Well, Noah is upset about his ma. I told you about his ma,

right? And I thought I'd make—"

"Jesus Christ, Aubrey. It's like you don't *want* to get a job."

"But I have a job."

Sean rolled his eyes. "A waitress at a bar."

I leapt to my feet, not wanting to have this argument yet again. "Sean, please, don't be mad at me. I'm sorry I forgot to tell you I'm working tonight. Let me make it up to you. This weekend?"

Sean gave me a long look. "Sunday."

But Sunday I'd planned to go to the O'Sullivans for Sunday lunch. Dammit. It'd been too long since I'd gone. Truth be told, I missed them. "I, um…"

Sean made a face and opened his mouth, likely to give out to me.

"Okay, Sunday. Yes, that works," I said quickly to appease him. I *had* forgotten to tell him not to come over.

Sean wouldn't let it go yet. "I could have stayed longer at work and worked on that presentation," he said, annoyance still in his voice.

"I said I'm sorry." I shoved a woolen hat over my unruly thick dark locks.

"Fine. I might as well head back into work." He turned to head out.

"Can you give me a lift then?" I asked.

The prestigious Dublin College of Music was a grand old Victorian-style building and where The Jar was located. It was technically a campus bar but was situated off the main road, so non-university students came to drink, play pool and listen to live gigs.

"Thanks, babe," I said to Sean as he turned into the circular drop-off point at the university's side entrance. "Sorry again for mucking you around this evening."

"You're lucky you're so cute," he said.

I was already partly forgiven.

He leaned over for a kiss. His lips were still cool from the outside.

"When will you be finished?" he asked, straightening.

On weeknights like this one, we closed at midnight. After cleanup and lockup, it meant I wouldn't be leaving till 1 a.m. "Probably one," I said.

Sean's lips pressed into a line. "It's not safe for you to be walking home that late."

"Noah's dropping me home," I said softly. Even though Noah lived out of the way from me, he always dropped me off after closing.

Sean's lips twitched at the mention of Noah's name. He never liked Noah. Noah wasn't his biggest fan either, and I didn't know why. Over the years I tried inviting them both out for drinks at our local bar, but they didn't seem to get on.

Correction…they didn't seem to even *want* to get on.

I'd long since given up and accepted that my boyfriend and my best friend would just have to live in two separate spaces in my life.

"Well, okay," I said, unclipping my seatbelt, "hope you get your presentation done."

"When we're married, I don't want you working at this bar anymore," Sean blurted out.

I turned back towards him with a snap. "What? Why not?"

Sean snorted. "Come on, Aubrey. Do you really want to be working at a bar for the rest of your life? I mean, I get why you have to now."

I worked there when I was a student. Now that my student visa had run out and I was only here on a tourist visa, I wasn't technically allowed to work. Noah let me work cash in hand.

I'd been trying to get a real job since I'd graduated with my business degree, but they always rejected me when they realized that they'd have to help me get a work visa if they wanted to hire me. I guess there were plenty of other Irish or European Union graduates with rights to work in Ireland already.

Damn not being an EU citizen.

Damn not being Irish.

That's why Sean proposed. Well, it wasn't really a proposal so much as it was a rational solution to the problem. He didn't get down on one knee. I didn't even have a ring. He just said "I suppose we could get married" over Chinese takeout one Sunday evening a few weeks ago.

The little girl romantic in me died a little every time I remembered I wouldn't have a wildly romantic proposal story to tell my kids. But that wasn't important, right?

What was important was that I got to stay in Ireland, the gorgeous country I'd fallen in love with since the day I arrived over four years ago.

"Well, you don't, do you?" Sean repeated, snapping me out of my head. "Want to be a barmaid all your life?"

My first reaction was, *what the hell is wrong with that if I'm happy?* But I didn't say it. Sean graduated with a business degree too, and now worked for a management consulting firm. He was one of their rising stars and would go on to do big things. I settled on business because I had no idea what I wanted to do with my life—still didn't.

"I guess not…" I said.

I hadn't really thought about it. The last four years of working at Noah's bar had been some of the best of my life. It'd be sad when I had to leave. Once I was married and had a visa to work here, I wouldn't have any problems getting a graduate job. For some reason, this prospect filled me with dread.

I gave Sean one more peck and hopped out of the car, running across the sodden sidewalk undercover. I waved at Sean as he drove off.

It hit me…everything was changing.

I was getting married.

Soon I wouldn't be working at The Jar anymore, I'd be working full-time for some company. And…

I wouldn't be able to see Noah as much. When I worked an office job, I'd be working days and he worked nights. I wouldn't have time to see his family, who had basically adopted me, either. I'd have to start going to Sean's family events. It was just Sean and his parents at their gatherings. Sean's parents were nice but very standoffish. Unlike Noah's mad family. I always got the impression that they didn't think I was good enough for their precious little son.

My heart twisted in my chest. Everything was about to change. I wasn't sure I liked it.

"Hey, girl," Candace called out from across the bar when I stepped into The Jar.

Candace was a tiny spitfire. Five foot nothing of passionate, outspoken whirlwind under a cloud of curly raven hair. Sometimes I was exhausted just watching her work the room, collecting empty glasses, stacking them in Jenga-like piles on her tray before carrying it above her head without dropping a single one, all with her huge, infectious smile plastered on her face. Her real name is Canciana but she introduces herself as Candace. When I asked her why, she said that Candace was her "English name." It was easier for people here to pronounce than Canciana. I noticed a lot of Brazilians do that. And there were a lot of Brazilians in Dublin.

I waved to her and headed to the staff room out back to dump my stuff in my locker.

The Jar was a dimly lit university bar, a wooden bar running along one end, a stage on the other with a dance floor in front, booths and tables in between. The walls were mosaicked with signed photos of the musicians who had drunk or played here, a *Who's Who* of Irish and international music fame. The bar's full name was Whiskey in the Jar, a song sung by The Dubliners, an Irish band popular in the seventies and eighties.

The Dublin College of Music had a quite a few famous musicians as teachers, and they always came into The Jar to jam.

In the backroom, I grabbed one of the black The Jar shirts in my size from the washed pile and slid it on instead of my jumper. On the back was printed "wack fall the daddy-o", a line from The Dubliners song that The Jar was named after. I'd originally made one for Noah as a laugh. But he loved them so much that he ordered a ton from me and made them part of the standard uniform. He insisted on paying me in cash. The gesture warmed my heart. I knew part of it was because he wanted to help me with my financial situation but knew I was too proud to take money from him for free.

I walked behind the bar and began to unstack the dishwasher of glasses, listening to Candace chatting away about her latest Tinder date fiasco.

"*Nossa, amiga!*" Which I've learned means *damn, girl* in

Portuguese. "Remind me again why you're not with *that man*?"

I glanced in the direction of Candace's stare.

Noah was walking out of the storeroom with a full slab of bottles hoisted over his shoulder, his biceps bulging from under his t-shirt.

Nossa, amiga indeed.

But I could never date someone like Noah.

He was too beautiful. Like, ridiculously otherworldly beautiful. The kind of beautiful that made every woman in the room tear her eyes off her boyfriend and mentally undress him from across the room.

I couldn't deal with having a boyfriend that women threw themselves at every friggin' day. I mean, even when we went out as friends, women hit on him right in front of me. We were *just* friends. But they didn't know that.

Noah was always gentlemanly in front of me. He always turned them down and apologized to me. But I knew his reputation for chatting up women. All the girls at my college had various stories of his playboy ways. Heartbreaker, they called him.

God of Thunder. That was another one of his monikers. Named as such because of his resemblance to Thor, the mythical god played most recently by Chris Hemsworth in the Marvel movies. And apparently…his ability between the sheets.

God of Thunder… My cheeks never failed to heat when I heard that nickname. I brushed it off as quickly as I could. I mean, who would ever want to see their gorgeous best friend naked, right? I mean, Noah was like a brother to me… Right?

Besides, he owned a bar, for God's sake. Drunk women plus hot bartender equals too much opportunity for him. No wonder he was a player. I didn't blame him. I just was never ever going to date him. Never.

Ever.

Besides, I was with Sean. Sean was cute and smart. Sure, he didn't make me laugh quite the way Noah did, and I never stayed up late talking with him like I did with Noah, but you can't have everything, right? I'd rather a loyal boyfriend who'd be *mine* rather than hot perfection who I could never trust. Right?

I caught Noah's eyes from across the bar and he smiled, his face lighting up. I knew his trademark dimple would be popping in his left cheek even though I couldn't see it.

I couldn't help the smile I returned to him.

Noah practically ran over looking like he hadn't seen me in weeks. Even though it'd been hours since I last saw him.

I laughed as he picked me up from the floor in a bear hug and rubbed his knuckles in my hair.

"Put me down, asshole."

"What? I missed you."

"Ugh, can you miss me from farther away though?" I joked.

"Thanks for earlier, Rey," he whispered in my ear. "I couldn't get through this without you."

My heart somersaulted in my chest, banging all my ribs. He lowered me and I slid down his body, trying to ignore how hard and strong it felt. I cleared my throat and took a step back. "I have something for you…" I said. "Thought it might cheer you up."

"Just seeing you cheers me up." Noah flashed me his trademark grin.

The smile with the dimple and the soft crinkles around his blue eyes that I could drown in. Was it any wonder he had a friggin' entourage of girls who came in here night after night waiting to capture his attention? A fresh batch appearing at the beginning of every college year.

I swear I heard Candace sighing in the background.

I rolled my eyes. Because I was totally immune to his grin. Totally. I swear. "Yeah, yeah. Save the sweet talk for ladies' night." I reached behind the bar and grabbed the thing I'd been working on all afternoon.

"A t-shirt?" he asked.

I flicked it open, holding it by the shoulders. "Do you like it?" I asked, not at all certain why I was acting so unsure.

Noah's eyes scanned the writing. He let out a laugh.

I relaxed. He liked it!

With one hand, Noah pulled his current t-shirt off.

I froze.

Candace let out a gulp so I was pretty sure she'd just swallowed her tongue.

Noah O'Sullivan, my best friend, had a firm chest and broad shoulders, tapering to a V and golden curls trailing down a perfect six-pack. He looked unreal. Like an immortal being trying to look like a human.

God of Thunder indeed.

He snatched the t-shirt out of my hands and pulled it over his naked torso.

Candace and I let out a collective sigh of disappointment as the most incredible body I'd ever seen in real life disappeared behind the t-shirt I'd printed that afternoon.

A picture of a boat with the words *Need a boat? I Noah guy.*

Noah slung an arm around my neck and pulled me in for a hug, his lips pressing above one eyebrow. "I love it, Rey. Love it."

I was never washing my forehead again.

He let go of me and I wobbled as I tried to find my own balance again, staring as Noah ambled off to the storeroom to…well, to do storeroom stuff, I guessed.

I was still stuck on two minutes ago when I'd seen more of my best friend than I'd ever seen before.

"*Nossa, amiga,*" Candance whispered again.

"Nossa, amiga," I agreed in a whisper.

Candace cleared her throat. I looked back to see Candace staring at me.

She raised one perfectly manicured eyebrow.

"What?" I asked, running a hand over my head. "Is my hair sticking up?"

"You two." Candace clenched at her heart and let out a sigh. "So cute."

My cheeks heated and I hoped to hell that they weren't obviously coloring. "We're just friends, Candace."

"Just friends. Yeah, okay."

No one seemed to believe that Noah and I were just friends. We were. *Just* friends. Really.

Aubrey

After work, Noah and I made our weekly pilgrimage to the twenty-four-hour convenience store to buy our lottery ticket for the weekly EuroMillions draw.

We'd been doing this since the first Saturday I stayed late after my first shift with Noah and we'd laughed our asses off over several pints.

As was our post-closing ritual, we grabbed a kebab from one of the late-night Turkish takeaways. It was too cold to eat in the car, which we often did during summer, so we headed to my apartment where we sat in my living room on cushions and stuffed our faces, the lottery ticket safely in Noah's pocket and our minds on what we'd do with the money if we won Friday's draw.

"I'd buy an apartment," I said between bites, in a low voice so not to wake my housemate. I stared around my flat, my eye catching on every crack and permanent smudge on the pale-yellow walls. They must have had a cut price on this particular shade of yellow because I swear to God, every rental apartment I'd ever been into in Dublin was this same horrible shade. My apartment was small, the insulation rubbish like most Irish apartments, but it worked for now and was cheap.

"I'd pay for my ma's heart surgery," Noah said in a quiet voice.

I swallowed my bite of lamb kebab hard, wincing as it went down like a stone. Here I was frivolously talking about buying apartments when Noah just wanted to keep his ma alive. I set my kebab aside, hunger forgotten, and scooted over so that I was right up against Noah's side. "What can I do?"

He gave me a half smile. "Just be here. That's enough." He wound an arm around my shoulders, pulling me against him.

Noah wasn't usually so affectionate, but he obviously needed the closeness today, so I laid my head on his chest, wrapping an arm around his waist. It felt good to be pressed up against his solid warm body. Really good. "There must be something I can do?"

He let out a sigh and rested his chin on my head, his breath ruffling my hair. "I don't even know what *I* should do."

I should be focusing on the problem. But all I could think was *goddamn, he is ripped*. I could feel the ridges of his six-pack along my forearm, the firmness of his pecs under my head. The biceps and sheer size of him have always been obvious with his clothes on and after his earlier shirtless display I knew exactly how defined his muscles were underneath.

What would he look like totally naked? I stole a look down his torso and my gaze came to rest on the bulge in his pants. My cheeks heated. God of Thunder indeed.

An idea struck me.

"You could do a calendar and sell them to raise money or something," I said before I could censor myself.

"A what?"

"You know, like one of those sexy fireman calendars."

He pulled back to look at me. "You think women would pay money for that?"

"Hell yeah." I followed a bunch of romance authors online because I liked their books and women always went crazy over the hot cover models. A lot of those models sold calendars and stuff. Noah could definitely give all of them a run for their money.

He lifted an eyebrow. "Would *you* would buy a calendar of me?"

I felt my cheeks heat even more. Ah shit. I was so busted.

Noah let out a chuckle. "You would."

"Well, yeah, to support you. And not *just you*," I spluttered, trying to make this all less embarrassing, "all your brothers. A four hot Irish brothers calendar or something. Girls would eat it up."

Noah pursed his lips, a sign that he was thinking. "You know, that's not half bad an idea."

I let out an internal sigh. Awkward line-crossing of our friendship averted. I grabbed the rest of my kebab and shoved it into my mouth to avoid any more embarrassing admissions.

Noah

"Policemen."

"Men in suits."

"Ooo!" Aubrey cried. "Irish cowboys. So hot right now."

I let out a chuckle. Sitting here joking around with Aubrey about sexy calendar themes made me feel lighter. She hadn't left my side and so we were still cuddled up under my arm. The world and all its problems felt so much smaller this way.

"We could wear actual cowboy hats," I said, taking her concept and running with it.

"*Only* cowboy hats. And boots." She laughed and let out a snort looking up to me.

My heart flipped when our eyes met. I wanted to lean down and kiss the shit out of her. But I couldn't.

Instead, I gave her shoulder a squeeze and said, "What would I do without you, Rey?"

She giggled in that girlish way that wrapped around the base of my spine. "I know. I'm pretty awesome."

I grinned. "You being stood up was the best thing that ever happened to me."

She rolled her eyes and pushed at my arm playfully. "Ass. You know Sean didn't really stand me up. He got the dates mixed up."

Four years ago, I spotted her sitting on one of the stools alone at The Jar glaring at her phone, obviously having been stood up. She was a pretty girl so I did what I did with every pretty girl I saw while I was working behind the bar. I went up to her, served her a drink on the house and made her laugh. But by the end of the night, we were *both* in stitches. She was a little drunk and I was completely drunk on her.

I'd walked her home after closing up and said goodbye to her at her front door. I'd cussed myself out all the way home and all the next day for not kissing her. For not claiming her then. I hesitated because…well, because I'd sensed even then that a kiss with her wouldn't just be *a kiss.*

Back then, I hadn't been ready for it. But you're never ready when you fall in love. That was the night I'd fallen in love with Aubrey Campbell. Even if I didn't realize it at the time.

If only I'd kissed her.

Maybe she wouldn't have accepted Sean's apology in the form of generic red roses. Sunflowers were her favourite flowers.

She wouldn't have gone on that date with Sean the next day. Maybe she wouldn't be his girlfriend.

Fiancée.

She was his fiancée now.

Maybe I wouldn't just be her *friend.*

If I could turn back time…

But I couldn't.

I tasted bitterness at the back of my throat. My fingers curled into Aubrey's flesh and I was seconds away from kissing her the way I should have four years ago. But that would ruin everything. She was with another man. Our friendship would be over if I ever made a move on her. I would lose her. Forever. The thought of not having Aubrey in my life, even as friends, was too painful to bear. More painful than having to love her in secret.

I pulled away from her suddenly, leaping to my feet. "I should go, Rey."

Her face flashed with disappointment and my heart ached. Because I knew there wasn't anything underneath that disappointment other than she didn't want her best friend to leave.

"Okay." She stood as well, wrapping her arms over her chest as if she were hugging herself, chewing her kissable bottom lip with her teeth. "I'll see you tomorrow."

I ran the hell out of there before I pulled her back into my arms.

How fucking ironic.

Noah O'Sullivan, one of Dublin's biggest players, in love with the only girl he couldn't have.

Later that night in bed alone, I couldn't get what Aubrey said out of my head.

Like one of those fireman calendars…

Ooo! Irish cowboys.

My business brain ticked over what it might cost to get one of those calendars done up. We'd need a website and a budget for marketing… Then I considered what kind of profit margin could we make per calendar…and how many calendars we'd have to sell…

Dammit, it wasn't enough. Even if I could convince all three of my brothers to get involved in something like this.

I'd be better off doing one of those charity auctions that sold me off for a "date night" with some rich woman.

I'd do it, too. I'd do anything to get my ma that surgery. Any-fucking-thing.

An idea struck me as I stared at the lottery ticket that Aubrey and I just bought sitting on my bedside table. An idea so damn crazy, it just might go viral.

Not a charity auction.

A lottery.

But…not just any lottery.

THE IRISH LOTTERY

Noah

"I have an idea on how to raise the money for ma's surgery."

My three brothers blinked back at me from their various places around my living room. I'd called an emergency O'Sullivan brothers meeting and they'd all come in a flash.

I was the eldest. Michael was next, only a year younger. He and I look most like our da, with sandy-blond hair and strong square jaws, aquiline noses and high foreheads. My eyes were blue like our ma's, while his were green. I kept my hair longer and as my ma always says, "unruly," while Michael's was cropped short and always styled. Michael ended up as legal counsel to some of Ireland's richest men. Which was why he was sitting in my living room in a tailored pinstripe suit, having just left work.

Darren was next at twenty-three, two years younger than Michael. He'd always been the strong, silent type and good with his hands. He was still in his work overalls, a smudge of oil on his cheek, having come straight from his garage that specialized in motorbike repairs.

Eoin was the youngest. He and Darren looked like our ma and had her dark hair and thick lashes, except their eyes were green like da's. He was lounging in one of my armchairs in his rugby sweats, blades of grass in his damp hair, so I knew he'd just come from practice. Eoin might only be twenty-one but he was a rising star in Irish rugby. He was getting a reputation off the field, too.

We were all so different in personality but we came together when it counted. I knew each one of these men had my back. I just hoped they'd agree with what I was about to propose…

"I'm going to sell tickets to a lottery," I announced.

I was met with blank stares.

I barreled on before anyone could interrupt, outlining my plan. The blank looks turned to frowns.

"Hang on. Tickets to what now?" Michael spoke first.

"To win a night with me," I said. "To do whatever they want."

"You mean…*sexually*?" Michael asked, his voice going higher than usual.

Darren let out a snort. "No, he's going to play bridge with them. Of course, sexually, dipshite."

Michael shot Darren a glare.

Darren just shrugged. Nothing rarely phased his cool façade.

"You're going to whore yourself out?" Eoin asked, his wide jade eyes on me.

"Well, jeez," I said, rubbing the back of my neck, "when you put it *that* way…"

"That," Eoin interrupted, "is fucking *deadly*. Getting paid to ride a hot rich chick…" He gyrated his hips.

I rolled my eyes. Trust Eoin to turn this into a joke. I grabbed one of the open bags of Tayto crisps so I could throw something at him.

Michael let out a snort. "It'd be more like some wrinkly old prune with cobwebs across her vag—"

I threw the cheese and onion crisp at Michael's head instead.

He tried to catch it in his mouth and missed.

"So what if she's old?" I said. "If I raise the money ma needs for this surgery…"

"Oh, shite," Eoin said, his eyes widening as if he just thought of something. "What the feck is ma going to say?"

"I won't tell her." I hated keeping where the money came from a secret. But it was better this way. Who cared about a little white lie if it kept her alive?

"But—"

"I'll wear a mask on the promo shots and make the winner sign an NDA."

"An NDA?" Eoin asked.

"A non-disclosure agreement, doofus. Even I know that," Darren said.

Eoin punched Darren in the arm, which kick-started a punch-off between them.

"You think you can sell enough tickets?" Michael asked me. He had a serious look on his face.

Out of the three of us, I figured he'd be the hardest to get on board with the plan. Even if he did get past the…controversial and extreme nature of the idea.

"I think so. I ran the numbers. If I sell each ticket for five euros, I'd only need to sell 50,000 to make enough to cover the operation."

Michael's eyes bulged out of his head. "Fifty thousand tickets? Where the fuck are you going to find fifty thousand women who are desperate enough to fork out five euros for a mere *chance* at winning you? I mean, yeah, you pull the chicks alright, or at least you did when you hadn't been dick-dazed by Aubrey yet—"

"Hey!" I protested.

"—but *fifty thousand* tickets?" Michael continued. "Shite on."

My shoulders fell, my idea souring before my eyes. Maybe this was a stupid idea. Maybe I was an idiot to think I could sell fifty thousand tickets to this fantasy lottery.

"What if we all do it?" Darren said.

We all turned to look at him.

"What?" I asked.

"If one O'Sullivan brother is tempting enough," Darren said slowly, "surely four O'Sullivan brothers will send ticket sales through the roof."

The rest of us O'Sullivan boys stared at Darren. Then at each other.

All four brothers.

One woman…

Not something we'd ever done before.

Jesus, not something we'd ever even considered before.

"What if they don't want all four of us in their fantasy?" Eoin finally piped up.

Darren shrugged. "Then they don't have to have all four. The winner gets to choose. Who, how many and what they want."

Winner's choice of four brothers.

Holy shit. My skin started to buzz the way it did when an idea had legs. This could work. This totally could work.

"An anonymous sex lottery," said Eoin, grinning.

I could tell he was already keen.

Although if his reputation was anything to go by, Eoin would sleep with almost anything in a skirt. "I'm so fucking in."

I looked at Darren. "Would you do it?"

"I suggested it, didn't I?" he said.

That meant yes.

Three out of four brothers were in. We could do it with three. It wouldn't be *as* appealing as four brothers, but still...

We all stared at Michael.

He paused. "I don't know... Jesus Christ, if anyone at the office ever found out. If my clients knew...""

"Mickey," Eoin said. "No one'll find out. They're signing that MBA thingy."

"*NDA*, ye eejit," Darren corrected.

Eoin stuck up his middle finger at him.

"Look," I said, turning to Michael, "if you don't want to do it, say no. No pressure."

Michael's face scrunched up. "It's not that I don't want to... But if it raises the money for ma's operation... Ah, feck it. I'll do it. But I'm drafting the NDA. And the terms and conditions."

I pumped my fist.

"Alright, Mickey!" Eoin leapt up from his seat and grabbed Michael in a half-hug, half-tackle.

"Get off me, you're wrinkling the Armani."

Eoin chuckled and ran his knuckles across Michael's head before darting out of the way of Michael's fist.

I nodded to my brothers, grinning as hope bubbled up inside me. We were all in this. The plan was crazy as shite but we were going to get our ma the surgery she needed. It was going to work.

The four of us drew up a plan.

Darren had built his own website for his mechanic shop and was decent at IT—anything mechanical, really—so he was going to be in charge of getting our lottery website up.

Michael would draft up the NDA and the terms and conditions of the contest.

Eoin found us the photographer who was a mate of his, sworn

to secrecy. The photographer didn't know what it was for, just that it was to raise money for our ma.

I was responsible for setting up the digital bank account that the money was all going to.

Today I had hope. Something that I didn't have yesterday.

But hope was a long way away from ma's surgery being paid for.

I felt tired and drained as I walked up to the door of The Jar a few days later. I took some comfort in the fact that it should be a quiet night and that it would be an easy shift. And Aubrey would be there. She always made the worst situations feel manageable somehow. Even now, the thought of her grin and easy humor eased some of the weight crushing down on my shoulders. I had to remind myself that she was someone else's fiancée. I had no right to think about her as anything other than a friend. Still, her beautiful smile and soft laugh snuck right back into my thoughts, quickening my steps, making my hand shake with anticipation as I lifted it to the handle of the door to The Jar.

"What's up, asshole?" Eoin's easy drawl broke through my thoughts.

I spun on my heel to find my youngest brother strolling up to me, dressed in black sweats—his formal sweats—and a blue jersey.

"What are you doing here?" I asked.

Eoin snorted and rolled his eyes. "You tell me."

I frowned. "What?"

"I got a message from Aubrey telling me to meet you guys here."

"We did, too." Darren appeared from the shadows, Michael following closely behind him.

What the hell was going on? I stood with all my brothers, the four of us glancing around at each other, unable to hold each other's eye contact for long. The last time we were all together was a few days ago when we decided we'd set up the lottery.

"Did you tell her?" Michael leveled an accusing look at me.

"Of course I didn't feckin' tell her."

"Then why are we here?" Darren asked.

Why indeed. I turned my back on my brothers and pushed through the front door of The Jar. My quiet night instantly went to hell as the packed room erupted into uncoordinated shouts of "Surprise!" Like a birthday surprise party gone wrong.

It wasn't my birthday.

My brothers spilled into The Jar around me.

"What is going on?" Eoin echoed my thoughts.

I picked Aubrey out of the throng of people, her radiant smile chasing away most of my apprehension. If she was smiling, then everything was okay.

With a few steps, Aubrey was in front of me. "I wanted to tell you, but I thought the surprise might be better," she said to me. "I knew you'd want to help and you have too much on your plate. I didn't want you to stress."

She hesitated as some guy I didn't recognize walked up and clapped me on the back while saying something roughly comforting about my mother and how she'd get through this. Why was this stranger saying things about my ma? What the heck was going on here? I glanced down at Aubrey and saw the worried look in her eyes. Like she was begging me to understand and not be mad.

"What's going on here?" I asked, more curious than anything else.

She moved her body towards me so we were shoulder to shoulder.

Eoin caught my eye and wiggled his eyebrows at Aubrey suggestively. Michael elbowed him, but he was looking too.

Darren still just looked stunned.

Ignoring them as best I could, I glanced down at Aubrey. She worried her lower lip between her teeth in a way that sent liquid adrenaline flowing through my veins, before releasing it and smiling widely at someone who walked past us.

"It's a fundraiser," she said, glancing up at me with serious eyes. "I wanted to help Ma and this seemed like a good way to do it. Remember, you've got a whole community of support behind you. People here know you, they love you, and with a little push, everyone can imagine being in your shoes. They want to help." Her eyes were shining with tears and…

Damn, it tore at me.

I yanked her into a hug and crushed her to my body, my arms as she clung to me.

She did this for Ma.

For my family.

For me.

"Thank you," I whispered, my words a paltry reflection of everything I was feeling. How did I ever deserve her in my life? How could I ever repay her? How could I even begin to tell her how much this meant to me? How much *she* meant to me?

She nodded against my chest. "I've been monitoring, too. We're not at capacity yet, the fire marshal won't fine us as long as not too many more people show up." She pulled away and glanced at the door with a worried look.

The level of responsibility she'd taken on didn't surprise me. I knew she was responsible, it was one of the main reasons I trusted her so much. Not only was she doing this fundraiser, she'd also taken local laws and regulations into account so we wouldn't get fined, and I had no doubt she'd made sure to abide by all of them. I wanted to thank her again, but before I could speak, she excused herself and slipped away into the crowd. I tracked her until an elbow caught me in the ribs and I grunted.

"Oh, damn," Eoin said, watching after Aubrey even though she was out of sight. "That woman's a keeper." He glanced up at me, arching an eyebrow in a clear challenge. "Either you make a move on her or I'm going to."

"The fuck you will," I growled, ready to lay his ass out. I didn't give a fuck that he was an up-and-coming Rugby champ. He had the weight, height, and muscle over me, but I'd get some good shots in before he knocked me out. I wasn't about to let him fuck around with the woman I loved. Even if she belonged to someone else. "She's *engaged*."

Eoin made a rude noise. "I don't give a damn. She's worth fighting for."

Darren stepped in between us, trying to put space between Eoin and me. Probably a good thing, too. I was half a second from giving my little brother the beatdown right here at a fundraiser for my ma.

"Have you considered telling Aubrey how you feel?" Darren asked me cautiously, watching like it wasn't the first time he'd caught a stray hook thrown between Eoin and one of us. It wasn't.

"Has everyone forgotten that *she's fucking engaged*?"

"I think Eoin's right," Darren said.

I noticed Eoin's smug nod as he crossed his arms.

"She's worth fighting for. Hell, she's fighting for our ma right now." Darren clasped a hand on my shoulder. "A woman like her might only come along once in a lifetime. Don't let her slip through your fingers."

Everything they were saying I knew. I felt it deep in my bones. Aubrey was one in a million. I regretted not kissing her for every day of our friendship. But she had picked me to be her *best friend*. She chose *him* to be her fiancé. I had no fucking right to try to mess things up between her and him, despite him being a right feckin' knob-end.

"What is this?" Eoin asked, giving Darren a disgusted look. "Emotion hour with Dr. Phil?"

At this, Darren dropped all pretenses and hit Eoin with a well-placed elbow.

My brother doubled over, muttering something about puking all over Darren's nice shoes.

"Over here!" Aubrey's cheerful voice rose over the din, and I saw her coming our way.

Without missing a beat, my brothers straightened, falling into their best behavior.

I noticed a man trailing behind Aubrey. I knew that face. How the hell…?

"She got Jason Reilly here?" Michael asked from behind me.

I locked on Aubrey's smile, unable to look away as she walked right up to us.

"You boys must know Jason Reilly of RTE," Aubrey said.

Us boys nodded in greeting at the local news anchor as Aubrey introduced us to Jason and the cameraman at his side, who I'd somehow failed to notice earlier. Ma would shite bricks if she were here. She loved Jason Reilly. *Such a handsome young man*, she always said with a wistful sigh. Did Aubrey think he was handsome?

"Jason's here to cover the event and raise awareness," she said, smiling widely up at me. I couldn't get the easy way she said his first name out of my head. It buzzed there like a bee even as she continued speaking. "The station set up a call-in line where people can call and donate from home, too!" Her voice hummed with excitement, her breaths coming out short and shallow.

I wanted to pull her into my arms and kiss her hard, the cameras be damned.

Instead, I forced myself to turn to Jason. "Thank you so much. We appreciate your help."

"When this beautiful young woman literally showed up at my office with this sad story and begged me to help, how could I resist?" Jason grinned at Aubrey.

I tasted something metallic on my tongue.

"I'd like to interview you as well," Jason said, obviously returning to a conversation they'd had before she led him over here.

"I can't be on camera!" Aubrey's cheeks turned pink.

"Sure you can. A beautiful girl like you talking about why we're having this fundraiser…the audience will eat it up."

His expression was unmistakable, and I wanted to punch the bastard right in his pretty face because I knew what he was thinking.

Aubrey chewed on her lip as Jason continued to try to coax her in front of the camera. I could see she was torn between wanting to do the best for this fundraiser and her own fierce need for privacy. I would not let her bow to this bastard, even if he was some big shot TV presenter.

I stepped between them, pushing Aubrey to my side. "She said no," I said to Jason, my voice coming out hard like stone.

Aubrey shot me an appreciative smile, and it felt like being hit with the warm summer sun full blast.

"Most people want their fifteen minutes of fame," Jason said with a sniff, brushing down his suit jacket.

Aubrey shook her head, her face pale. "Not me."

"Neither do I, but I'll get in front of the camera for my ma," I said. "Boys, you up for it?" I directed this question to my brothers.

The three of them nodded.

Aubrey's gaze shifted back to me and I was stuck on the slight curve at the corners of her lips and the way she tilted her head back, exposing her throat. Everything about this woman drove me mad.

"Noah?"

"Huh?" I asked.

"Jason's ready to start the interview," Aubrey said.

I had to concentrate on the camera, otherwise my crush would be broadcast for all of the country to see. "Now?" I asked, feeling my brothers rallying at my sides.

Jason Reilly nodded and waved at the cameraman to get into

position.

Suddenly, my mouth went dry.

Aubrey was in front of me, fussing at my collar. "You'll be great," she said.

I nodded, somehow having lost my voice. I'd have to find it again before the camera started rolling.

"This will help the fundraiser, I promise."

Hearing her promise me anything in that breathless, excited voice could potentially ruin my ability to convince her—and myself—that I only saw her as a friend.

She stepped away from me and I felt her loss immediately. She stood by the cameraman's side with a thumbs up and I heard Jason call *action.*

Together with my brothers, we worked the interview as best we could.

Michael and Eoin knew how to be in front of a camera and it showed. I was worried I was a bit stiff through the interview, but Darren really struggled, finally settling on staying quiet and standing near the back.

"So, Noah, it was your…girlfriend," Jason said, glancing at Aubrey as if asking her, *please tell me you're single and this guy isn't with you,* "Aubrey, who organized this whole fundraiser as a surprise. She must be pretty special."

I looked over at Aubrey, our gazes locking and my breath was stolen.

I should correct him. Aubrey wasn't my girlfriend.

Her cheeks flushed and she tore her eyes off me. But she didn't correct him, either.

Why didn't she correct him?

"Aubrey is the greatest woman I know," I said truthfully, still looking at her instead of at the camera or Jason. I infused my words with all the love that I felt but could never say. "I am the luckiest man alive to have her in my life."

Aubrey

The guys had finished up their interview and the live telethon had finally picked up a bit of steam, or so Jason had confided in me. I scanned the busy bar. Several local bands had offered to play for free and people were dancing. I could hear people excited about the raffle all around me, all hoping to win some prize or another from the local businesses that had donated. The electric buzz in the air was *exciting*, but I couldn't seem to settle in and enjoy myself.

I frowned down at my phone for the thousandth time in the

past minute. Still no response.

Me: Where are you?

I hit send, despite the previous half-dozen messages in the same vein that hadn't been answered. Maybe this time Sean would actually message me back.

Maybe there was another reason he wasn't answering. Maybe his phone was dead. Or maybe he'd left it on silent after a meeting. Maybe messaging wasn't the way to reach him. With a glance around, I noticed everything was going just fine without me, so I slipped away towards the staff room at the back to call him instead.

As it rang, I took a deep breath and let it out slowly like I was decompressing and grabbed at the back of my neck with my free hand like I could rub away the weary tension there. I couldn't. The ache persisted and began to creep up like it was going to turn into a full-blown headache. I said a silent prayer that it wouldn't.

Sean answered on the second ring with a surprisingly curt tone that cut me to the bone.

"Where are you?" I asked.

"I'm busy with work right now."

His abruptness and downright rude tone of voice stunned me. "You promised to be here," I said and cringed. I promised myself I'd never be one of those nagging girlfriends, but lately, that's all I felt like.

I'd reminded Sean about Noah's fundraiser yesterday. I'd even asked him to set an alarm a half hour before so he'd have enough time to get ready and get here. I needed his support; I'd never done anything like this before.

He let out a sigh. "It wouldn't make a difference if I was there. The fundraiser won't make more money if I show up."

"That's not the point," I said, exasperation coloring my tone. That's not why I asked him to come in the first place. I wanted him here for *me*. I was going to marry this man. I needed to trust him to have my back. To be there when I needed him most. Did he not understand that I asked him to come to support *me*, not Noah? This was important to *me*. Wasn't I important to him?

"Never mind" I said, forcing my voice into a semblance of calm. "When will you get here?"

"I have too much work to do."

My heart dropped. "So you're not coming at all?" I nearly shrieked.

"I'm sure *your boyfriend*, Noah, would prefer it if I didn't show up." There was a bitterness in his voice that I could not ignore.

My boyfri—?

Sean must have seen or heard the live interview that Noah had done. He must have heard the newscaster call me his girlfriend.

Guilt stung at my cheeks. Noah hadn't corrected him. But neither had I.

"That was a mistake!" I cried. "The newscaster assumed—"

"Whatever," Sean's annoyed voice cut in. "I don't have time for this right now, Aubrey. I have more important things to do." The line went dead in my ear.

Hurt, anger and the unmistakable sting of guilt swirled around me as I glared at my cell phone.

Sean told me he'd be here. He wasn't. He'd let me down when I needed him. And instead of being understanding and apologetic, he'd gone right to being a dick for no reason and attacked my best friend. My best friend who was struggling to figure out how to save his mother's life. Did my fiancé even have a heart?

It's not like Noah went out of his way to be nice to Sean. But he was never rude.

I hated that my fiancé refused to even try to get along with my best friend.

Yeah okay, he had a right to be pissed that Jason had told the country that I was Noah's girlfriend, but it was a mistake. An honest assumption. If Sean had been here in the first damn place like he'd promised, Jason wouldn't have made that assumption.

"Everything okay?"

I jolted at the rich, warm sound of Noah's voice. Turning on my heel to face him, I nodded, my mouth feeling very dry as he studied me from the doorway. And something in me cracked. I shook my head. "No," I whispered, suddenly needing to lean on someone. Or fight with someone. I wasn't sure. Mixed up and angry, I struggled inside. "Why are you here?"

"Well," he said slowly, "this *is* my bar."

His usual dry humor didn't help my bad mood. "No, *here*." I swept my hand across the space between us, clearly asking him why he'd snuck up on me and startled me. The fundraiser was happening in the main part of the bar, so why was he back here with me?

"I was looking for you." His brows narrowed with obvious concern. "Rey, what's wrong?"

"Nothing."

He raised an eyebrow.

"Everything."

The other eyebrow joined the first.

I let out an annoyed growl and dropped my phone into my purse. "Sean and I had a fight. I *don't* want to talk about it."

The pained look on Noah's face dissolved some of my anger. I had no right to take it out on him. It wasn't Noah's fault Sean was being a dick. I took a deep breath and tried to calm the fuck down. I wouldn't let Sean ruin my night. I wouldn't let him screw up this good thing I'd done with this fundraiser. After all, this night was for Noah, his brothers and most importantly, their ma.

I forced a smile to my face but it felt more like a grimace. "I'm sorry. Sean told me he'd be here and—"

I stopped talking as Noah lifted a hand and spoke in a gentle tone. "You don't owe me an explanation. You don't want to talk about it, that's fine. We won't talk about it. In fact, we don't have to talk at all." His blue eyes sparkled with mischief as a familiar song vibrated through the walls: "Lime in the Coconut".

One of those songs he and I belted out in the car.

"Oh, no," I said, backing up as he stalked towards me, his hands out, his hips already twitching to the jungle beat.

"Oh, yesssss."

I laughed as he caught me and dragged me out of the staff room. I followed, protesting only half-heartedly as he led me onto the dance floor. He turned to face me and yelled out, "I said Doctor!" into a fake microphone.

He held the "microphone" to my mouth. I shook my head and pinned my lips shut.

"Aw, come on, Rey. *I said Doctor!*"

That pouty face. Those puppy dog eyes. How could I resist? I yelled out the next lyrics on a laugh.

With a grin he began to wiggle his hips to the beat, acting as silly as we did when we were alone. I couldn't hold back a giggle at how utterly ridiculous he was. As the music sped up, he continued to move, showing how surprisingly agile he was for such a big, built guy. All those hours in the gym hadn't turned him into a lumbering brute, no. He was muscular, but he could *move*. His heavy grace was impressive. The boy could dance. It didn't surprise me; Noah was one of those guys who somehow managed to be good at everything he tried. Or almost everything. I knew he couldn't skate at all and felt like anything on the ice was *of the devil*; something he'd mutter under his breath before flashing me a grin that was so hot it could melt any rink he visited.

Noah and I had never sung or danced together in public. Irish men did not dance, or so I was told repeatedly by more than one O'Sullivan brother. But here Noah was, in front of all these people, sober as anything, ready to put his pride on the line to cheer me up.

And it was working.

My anger and thoughts of Sean slipped away as we shook our bodies around each other, bumping our hips, laughing, yelling out for the doctor. Everything faded away. All my worries. All my stress.

This was why Noah O'Sullivan was my favorite human in the entire world. He was always there for me. My heart squeezed with gratitude for him.

God, if only he wasn't such a player, he'd be a great boyfriend. The best.

I quickly shut down that line of thinking as the song ended.

On the dance floor Noah arched an eyebrow at me as if silently asking me what was going to come next. I lifted my shoulders a tiny bit. I had no idea what the cover band would play. We didn't have to wait long before the music started up again. This time it was a slow song—"1000 Times" by Sara Bareilles. I knew because I'd listened to it over and over. It was a song about loving a friend that didn't love you back.

There was a look in Noah's eyes I didn't understand, some glimmer like he recognized the song. No, that wasn't quite right. It was something deeper than recognition. Like he *felt* it.

He blinked and it was gone. I couldn't help but wonder if I'd imagined it.

All around us, couples embraced and began to sway slowly to the sad music. Would we…? I looked back at Noah. He was staring right back at me like he was unsure as to what to do next. Slow dancing with my best friend? Holding each other close? Some small part of me tugged forward, but I pulled back. A part of me realized that if we did this, something might change forever. Everything was already set to change. I wasn't ready for it.

But I couldn't just stand here. It was getting awkward. With every second that passed, it became stranger.

A nervous chuckle burst out from me. "I need some air."

He nodded, looking both relieved and disappointed somehow. I didn't have a chance to think about it too much. He took my hand, once more leading me through the mess of people simply enjoying themselves for the best cause. I couldn't help but smile when it became clear where we were going. We slipped out onto the fire escape, alone.

Noah

The soft moonlight bathed Aubrey's elegant profile as she stared out over the Dublin rooftops, seemingly lost in thought. There was a vulnerability to her that made me want to pull her close and just hold her. I wanted to touch her as freely as the light was doing. I wanted to open up her mind and collect all her thoughts for myself. To guard her precious heart from any pain.

I took this moment to stare freely at her as the muted sounds of the fundraiser carried on behind us. The fundraiser that she'd organized in secret for my family, my ma, for me.

I didn't think I could love her more than I already did. But once again, she'd proven me wrong.

She glanced at me then back to the sky before doing a double take. "What?" she asked, a smile tugging the corners of her lips as if she'd noticed I'd been staring at her. Not that I tried to hide it.

I shrugged. "Nothing."

Aubrey smirked at me. "Liar," she said softly, but didn't push.

How would she react if I just spilled my secrets out to her? If I lay my heart out for her to do with what she may? Admission gathered on my tongue. "You look beautiful tonight," I blurted out.

She let out a nervous chuckle. "Liar," she repeated.

"I wouldn't lie to you."

She blushed and punched my shoulder lightly, probably to try and lighten the mood. "Thanks." Her hair was swept up and pinned back in some elegant thing.

My hands itched to pull out the pins holding her locks back and watch her hair tumble freely around her face.

She let out a sigh and some of the pensiveness from before crept back over her face. "What should I do about Sean?" she asked.

Even as my hope perked up, I told myself to be careful. "What do you mean?" I asked.

"He promised he'd be here tonight but…"

He wasn't.

My hands curled into fists. Asshole. How could Sean ever let her out of his sight?

"I mean, I know career is important, but I always thought that I'd end up with a man who'd ultimately put me first. You know?"

I nodded. I agreed with her. Work was just there to fund the life you were creating with the ones you love.

"And with this upcoming visa deadline…" She trailed off. She didn't need to finish her sentence. I knew what she was trying to weigh up. She'd be giving up more than a marriage if she gave up Sean.

She turned to me with her whole body. "What do you think I should do?"

Here was my chance. A chance to water the seeds of doubt already sown in her mind over Sean.

I opened my mouth to…

I couldn't do it. Not even to have her for myself. I'd never forgive myself if I had a hand in breaking up a relationship, even one as wrong as hers was with Sean. "I can't answer that for you," I said, the words feeling thick on my tongue as I swallowed down the words I really wanted to say.

Don't marry him.

Marry me.

She shrugged and put on a smile that didn't reach her eyes. "I'm sure it's nothing. He's just been stressed lately with work. He's a good guy, really."

Fuck. I choose my next words carefully. "I'm sure you'll make the right decision."

"Ugh," she said with a sigh. "Sucks to be an adult sometimes." She nudged me. "Thanks for making adulting less sucky."

I nudged her back. "Right back atcha, Rey. Thank you for doing all this." We could still hear the music playing and the laughter, the dull roar of voices on the fire escape. "You're kinda the best friend a guy could have."

I saw something flicker in her eyes, a tiny flash that looked almost like hurt but it was gone before I could decipher it.

She placed a hand over mine. "I hope this works. I hope it's enough to cover Ma's surgery. I know how stressed out you've been without a plan to raise the money."

But I had a plan. A plan that involved selling my body for money. A plan I didn't tell her about. Guilt threaded through me, her hand suddenly feeling like it was burning my skin.

Aubrey smiled, unaware of the turmoil growing in me. "It's the least I could do after everything you and your family have done for me."

I couldn't go through with the lottery. I couldn't sleep with a stranger.

The reason why was staring me in the face.

She leaned into me, her attention returning to the moon and stars as we stood on the fire escape, listening to the music playing inside. It felt right being her with her like this. I could feel her warmth and smell the sweet, clean scent of her vanilla perfume mingled with her coconut shampoo. Hope surged in me.

This fundraiser would work. I could cancel the lottery and tell Aubrey the truth—that I was in love with her. That I've loved her since that first night when she drank too much and made me laugh like no one ever had before her. Actually, screw waiting. I opened my mouth, ready to tell her the truth now. "Aubrey—"

The fire escape door burst open. Candace stuck her head out. "Hope I'm not interrupting anything."

I bit down my annoyance and aimed for nonchalant. "We're just getting some air. What's up?"

"Time to announce how much money was raised!"

Aubrey looked at me and we both grinned. My heart soared, certain that all our troubles would be over and I could tell Aubrey the truth about how I felt about her.

"Anda logo, amigos!" Candace waved us in hurriedly.

Together, we headed inside, my nerves jangling. Candace took her place on the stage in front of the microphone as Aubrey and I stood to one side.

Eoin, Michael and Darren were clustered on the other side of the stage. They spotted us coming in from the back. Michael raised an eyebrow at me. Eoin waggled his suggestively.

I wanted to slap them both. Thankfully, Aubrey's focus was all on Candace.

"Attention, everyone," Candace's voice echoed through the loudspeaker. "It's time to announce the total amount pledged."

The band had stopped playing and the crowd had fallen silent in anticipation, their attention turned to the stage. Candace's eyes shone with excitement as she got ready to read the number that had been given to her.

Aubrey's hand slipped into mine and her warm fingers linked with mine. It felt right to be standing there like this, holding her hand. I could almost believe she was mine. My girlfriend, not just my best friend.

"And the total amount pledged," Candace said, taking a deep breath and waiting a second for full effect. I tensed up. Just say the number already. "Is 16,730 euros!"

Cheers erupted from the crowd.

Aubrey turned to me, her eyes wide and excited, anticipating my reaction.

I put on a thrilled face and grabbed her in for a hug, even as I tried to hide my sinking feeling that fish-hooked my heart and dragged it straight to my toes. It was a good amount of money, but not nearly enough to pay for Ma's treatment.

I couldn't cancel the lottery.

I couldn't tell Aubrey how I felt yet.

Because I was going to sleep with a stranger for money.

I had to wait and tell Aubrey after the fact. And I would tell her. As soon as everything was said and done, I'd come clean and tell her the truth. All of it, all the ugly bits. And I knew she'd forgive me. I hoped she'd forgive me. She'd understand that I would do anything, *anything* to save my ma. She'd understand. She had to. Right?

THE IRISH LOTTERY

Noah

The day of the lottery photo shoot was upon us.

I was nervous as all hell. And sore. I'd gone to Gallagher's Gym earlier that day and smashed myself in order to pump up my muscles for the shoot that night.

Once we did the shoot it was all systems go. It all felt too real. Jaysus, were we really doing this? Could I have sex with a stranger? I mean, shite, I'd had my fair share of one-night stands, but I'd never *shared* a woman. Never had sex for money.

It wasn't for money, I reminded myself, it was for Ma's heart operation.

"Are you okay?" A soft feminine voice came from beside me.

I spun to find Aubrey staring at me with a funny look on her face. "What?" I asked.

She raised an eyebrow. "I said 'are you okay'?"

"Yeah. Yes. Grand."

The fundraiser was days ago. Since then I'd barely spent time alone with Aubrey. Sean had taken her out on her day off to apologize and I was spared the need to pretend I was too busy to see her. Honestly, I could barely stand to look at Aubrey with everything I was keeping from her. I could swear that my secrets were showing through my face. The other half of me was worried I'd blurt out something stupid, like...*I love you.*

I'd managed to avoid being alone with her. Until now.

"What do you need, Rey?" I tried to keep the bite out of my voice.

She crossed her arms over her chest. "You were taking forever, so I came in to see whether you needed any help."

Right. I came into the storeroom for a slab of Orchard Thieves Cider bottles. Instead I'd been staring at nothing for God knows how long. My head was all over the place. "I'm grand," I repeated.

Aubrey let out a snort and patted me on the shoulder.

"Alrighty then. I'll leave you to it." She turned and walked out of the storeroom.

She knew I was lying.

I let out a long breath that shifted my hair off my forehead. I hated keeping secrets from her. Every time she was around me, I wanted to blurt out what my brothers and I were doing. But I couldn't. I didn't want her to know because…I knew my reputation as a player. Once upon a time it would have been accurate. Mostly. People tended to exaggerate. I didn't think I'd ever kept anything this big from her…

Since I realized I was in love with her.

THE IRISH LOTTERY

Aubrey

Noah was *not* grand. He hadn't been grand for days, jumping every time his phone pinged, hiding his screen when he read his messages. I knew better than to push. He would tell me what was up when he was ready. Ugh, he was just taking longer than usual to be ready.

Maybe he was seeing someone. My heart squeezed. That would explain his secrecy lately. And the fact that he and I hadn't hung out since the fundraiser. But...he didn't have that smug excitability you get when you start seeing someone new.

It was probably to do with his mother. My heart gave another squeeze. Noah and I hadn't won last week's EuroMillions draw, so her heart surgery was still a distant hope. When pushed, Noah admitted quietly to me that the money raised hadn't been enough. I'd failed him.

I was still frowning when I approached the bar where Candace was wiping down the counter.

She looked up past my shoulder and froze. "*Nossa*, Aubrey Jennifer Campbell, have I died? Tell me I have died and gone to His Father in heaven. Hyyyyyyyayaya." Candace pretended to wobble on her legs while fanning herself.

"Candace," I said in alarm, "are you okay?"

She ignored me and continued to drool at something across the room.

I turned my head to find the three O'Sullivan brothers, Michael, Darren and Eoin walking into The Jar.

They must be here to pick up Noah. He mentioned he was leaving early.

I waved the three boys over and heard Candace choking from my side. "Stay cool, Candace," I said out of the corner of my mouth.

The three boys sauntered over and I walked around the bar to greet them all with a quick hug.

Candace squeaked as they greeted her too, before she spluttered some excuse about needing to wipe down tables.

I giggled to myself. She'd *already* wiped down the tables.

I got why she was intimidated. The O'Sullivan boys were all around six foot, just like Noah. All gorgeous, plump-lipped and had thick hair. All well-built, their bodies shown off by their jeans and fitted jumpers. All four of them trained regularly at Gallagher's Gym.

"You guys must be up to something naughty." I eyed them all with a grin. "You all scrub up well. You don't even have any oil marks on you, Darren!"

Darren matched my grin. "Why thank you, my lady."

"He actually took a shower," joked Eoin.

Darren punched his arm.

Michael let out a snort. "Children."

"Where are you boys going?" I interrupted before the punching turned into a brawl.

"Boys' night," Eoin said as he flashed me his cheeky trademark grin, his dimple showing.

"Uh-huh, and what's in the cards for boys' night?"

All three brothers spoke at once.

"Movies," said Michael.

"Pub," Darren said.

"The zoo," said Eoin.

I frowned.

The zoo? I caught Darren mouthing to Eoin.

What? Eoin mouthed back.

Michael was the only one who remained unfazed. "What my brothers and I are trying to say is that we're going to the pub, then the movies then…er, the zoo."

My frown deepened. "I didn't think Dublin Zoo was open this late."

"They aren't," Michael said, his voice slowing. "Right. Yeah, I suppose it's just the movies and the pub then."

The boys were *so* lying. They obviously didn't want me to know where they were going. Which meant they were probably going to that exclusive millionaires' club Michael was a member of, not that he was a millionaire himself, at least not yet, but because he had millionaire clients and one of them gifted him access. *An Seomra Ban* it was called—Michael always corrected my pronunciation to *awn showm-ra bahn*—which meant *The White Room* in Irish.

You had to be invited to join. The details of what went on within those walls were kept well-guarded.

"There he is. Finally," Eoin said, looking over to where Noah was walking out of the storeroom towards us, carrying a box of O'Hara's pale ale on his shoulder.

I found myself staring at the bulge of Noah's bicep as he lowered the box onto the counter behind the bar. I shoved that thought away and kept my face neutral. At least I tried. I found Darren watching me, a curious tilt to his lips.

"You took your time getting ready, princess," Eoin ribbed Noah, tapping his watch. "We said 9 p.m. on the dot."

"Settle yourself, boss," Noah said. "It's only 9:07."

"Are you coming dressed like that?" Michael said, eyeing him over.

Noah looked down at himself. He was in his usual ripped jeans and black band t-shirt, this one with *The Untouchables* written across the front. "What's wrong with what I'm wearing? It's not like—" He cut off, his eyes glancing to me.

I rolled my eyes. "Yeah, yeah, secret squirrel. Don't tell poor Aubrey about the terrible things you're off to do because her innocent female constitution can't handle it."

"Rey, you know it's not like that," Noah said, his voice softening.

I lifted a finger to him. "I'll have you know, mister, that I can be just as devious and salacious as you lot. Maybe even more." I shot him a wink and fist pumped internally when Noah looked fit to burst.

"Alright. We best be off." Darren grabbed Noah by the shoulders and steered him towards the door before Noah could respond.

Michael and Eoin followed them, waving goodbye to me as they went.

"You're in charge, Rey," Noah called back over his shoulder.

"Okay," I yelled back. "I'll try not to have any orgies on your bar counter."

I swear I heard Noah choking over the sound of his brothers laughing.

Noah

Once we got over standing around in just our jeans, the photo shoot went off without a hitch. The photographer was professional and we'd booked out a private studio so the lighting and plain white backdrop was already set up. We managed to get a stack of usable shots in less than an hour. Michael convinced us to spend the rest of the night at this exclusive club he was a member at, An Seomora Ban—The White Room—located on the top floor of a building that overlooked the River Liffey that ran through the centre of Dublin. It was a Saturday night, after all.

I'd only ever been in there once before. It was one of those poncy places that had thousand-euro designer jackets in racks ready for you to wear if you didn't have one.

"Damn, this suit is nice," Eoin said as he ran his hands down the pinstriped suit jacket.

Darren let out a whistle as he checked himself out in one of the full-length mirrors that covered the walls of the lobby area. He looked great in a jacket that fit his wide shoulders perfectly and buttoned up around his waist like it was tailored for him. "I usually can't get a jacket to fit like this. Where would you get one of these?"

"Try Armani and the monthly paycheck of one of your mechanics," I said.

Darren's eyes bulged out of his head. He stared down at the jacket in awe before looking back to the mirror. "Hey…" he whispered. "Do you think they'll miss it if I walk out with it?"

Michael shot him a dirty look as he let the attendant help him with his own navy-blue jacket.

I slipped on the jacket the attendant had picked out for me, dark grey wool and double breasted. Damn. This was lovely. And fit perfectly. "Maybe if we knock out the attendant…" I whispered to Darren.

Eoin was the only one of us that didn't look impressed. "I look like a feckin' eejit."

I let out a snort as the attendant shot him a startled look. It had been the first time that the older man had shown any sort of emotion since we got here. He'd probably been trained to act inconspicuously.

"You look smart," Michael said with a frown. "It's nice to see you out of those damn hoodies and sweats you always wear."

Eoin's jacket was a light blue colour. It fit him perfectly and made him look older than his twenty-one years.

My chest squeezed. Our little Eoin was a man now.

Eoin placed his hands on his hips. "I look like one of those rich bastards named Reginald who wears boat shoes and smokes cigars."

"What the hell is wrong with cigars?" snapped Michael.

Darren and I hid our laughter. Michael loved his Cubans. And his collection of boat shoes.

I clasped my hands on Eoin's shoulders. "Come on, Eoin, you don't look poncy."

"Nah," interjected Darren. "More like…a knob.

"A knob-end even," I said.

Eoin, Darren and I stared at each other before bursting out into laughter.

Michael rolled his eyes as he herded us into the club, but even he had a smile to his lips.

The club took up four entire floors according to Michael.

Apparently, there were private ensuite bedrooms for guests to stay in, a sauna and gym, a Michelin-starred restaurant that also did room service if you required a caviar bruschetta or lobster bisque at two in the morning and didn't want to get out of bed. There was also a private rooftop garden area that was open only when the weather was warmer. Supposedly. Us mere mortals, or "club guests", were only allowed as far as the bar area.

Even so, the bar area was swanky enough.

I stared around us as a gorgeous hostess in a wine-colored cocktail dress led us to our table.

An oil sheik would feel at home here: gold-leaf vines snaking around grand columns, leather and marble everywhere, and a huge crystal and gold chandelier dripping from the center where a stiff-necked man sat at a glossy grand piano, playing lounge classics. Waitresses in classy cocktail dresses carried slim trays of dew-rimmed drinks.

The bar was dotted with low tables clustered with leather armchairs and curved booths that gave guests some semblance of privacy. Floor-to-ceiling windows overlooked the river and the Dublin city lights shone like diamonds below, the Dublin spire like a giant needle over the other side of the river. Balcony areas overlooked the whole bar.

"Holy shite," Eoin said, his voice echoing just a little too loudly. "This place looks like Rockefeller hurled up all over it."

Darren chuckled.

"If you're just going to embarrass me, I'll make you leave,"

Michael hissed under his breath.

"Be cool, Eoin," I said, even though I was trying hard not to gape. The sheer opulence of the place made me a little dizzy. I guessed this was how the other half lived.

We were seated at a low table in a corner as the hostess handed us all menus and flashed a brilliant pearly white smile before slipping away with promises to send a waitress over in a few minutes.

I looked around at the other club members hoping to see either Danny or Declan. Danny O'Donaghue from The Untouchables was someone I'd call a friend. He was back in town last I heard. He and his best friend, Declan Gallagher, would be the only people I'd have a chance at knowing in here. Declan Gallagher was the current world number 1 MMA fighter, who happened to own the gym where I was a member.

"Holy shite, Mick," Darren said as he stared at the menu. "Do they have a whiskey here that's under three hundred quid a bottle? I could fit my bike out with new tires for that."

"Relax, I have a tab," Michael said.

Darren raised an eyebrow at Michael. "If you have that kind of money to throw around for gargle, why the hell are we doing this lottery shite to raise money for Ma?"

Michael flushed. "Okay, fine. It's the company's tab."

"You're not going to get in trouble with the boss if you put our drinks on the tab, are ye, Mick?" I asked.

Of all the brothers, my relationship with Mick had never been as close as my relationship with Darren and Eoin. But he was still my brother and I loved him to bits, even if he was a bit of an ass sometimes. I didn't want him to lose his job over a couple of glasses of drink.

Michael waved his hand. "I have a spending budget. My partners want me to come here at least once a week and schmooze with the other members. Besides, your money's no good here. They don't take cash or card. It all goes on the member's tab."

"Hello, gentlemen. My name is Delaney Evans. I'll be your server for this evening." A soft melodic tone interrupted our conversation. She had an accent, American, I think.

As she took our orders, I noticed Eoin, Darren and Michael all giving her their most charming smiles.

I looked at her closer. Delaney was a shapely girl, her black dress clinging to her curves, hem to just above her black-stockinged knees, the collar scooping just across the start of her generous cleavage, all enough to be sexy, not too much to be trashy.

Her face was a pleasant sweetheart shape framed by thick dark locks that fell down to her mid-back, enough of a tan in her skin which clued me in to her mixed heritage, cute nose, soft cheekbones, dark eyes, but it was her mouth that drew your eye. Painted in a sinful vixen red, her plump, wide lips could rival Angeline Jolie's. It turned her features from cute to downright sexy.

She didn't do anything for me, though.

I gave her my order—a Jameson and ginger ale—and handed her my menu with a polite smile. After taking everyone's orders, she sashayed off, Eoin and Michael drooling down their chins as they watched her.

I caught Darren looking at me instead. "Attractive girl, Delaney is, don't you think?"

I blinked. What was he getting at? "Yeah. Sure."

"Not as hot as Aubrey though, is she?" Darren winked at me.

What the—?

Before I could protest, Michael let out a strangled kind of noise. "Don't look now, but up over there," he said, "are none other than…Ronan O'Hara, Kane McCabe and Shay Kavanagh!"

Of course, we all looked up. There on the balcony were three men in business suits leaning over the balcony.

"I said don't look, for God's sake," Michael hissed.

Too late for that.

Not that the three gentlemen in question were paying us any attention. They were too busy watching someone on the floor. I glanced in the direction of their stares and my eyes fell upon a familiar curvy girl with a distinctive walk.

They were watching Delaney Evans, our attractive waitress.

"Who are they?" Eoin asked.

"Who are—?" Michael spluttered. "Only three of Ireland's

richest men."

I gazed back at these three wealthy men. They'd be in their late twenties or early thirties. I watched them talking, their hands animated before they laughed and shook hands with each other. Whatever they just agreed upon…it had something to do with Delaney. I almost wanted to warn her when she came over but…what the hell would I say? *"Hey, those three men were just staring at you and then they shook hands, so watch out?"* I'd sound like a lunatic.

"O'Hara is hotel royalty," Michael continued in a hushed reverent voice. "His family owns the Merrion luxury hotel chain that's all throughout Europe. McCabe is a business investor, Europe's answer to the US's Warren Buffet. And Kavanagh is one of the largest developers in Europe." Michael let out a wistful sigh.

Darren snorted. "Put your hard-on away, Mickey. You're drooling."

Michael shot Darren a glare. "If I could get even one of them to sign over one percent of their legal work with my firm, I'd…I'd make my career."

"Well, go then," I said. "We'll mind your whiskey if it arrives while you're gone."

Michael glanced up, chewing his lip as us three boys sang out words of encouragement.

"Fuck it." Michael smacked the table with the flat of his palm. "They're just men. I'm a man—"

"Questionable," muttered Darren with a chuckle.

Michael either didn't hear Darren or was ignoring him as he continued his pep talk to himself. "—why wouldn't they talk to me? Why wouldn't they want to do business with me?"

"That's the spirit!" I cried, lifting an invisible glass.

Michael leapt to his feet, brushed down his jacket and strode across the room, assumedly to wherever the stairs were to get to the balcony.

"Ten bucks says he strikes out," Darren said as soon as Michael was out of earshot.

"Daz, come on," cooed Eoin. "Michael deserves a little respect." He paused. "At least bet twenty bucks."

"If only I could find someone stupid enough to take that bet," Darren said, before the two of them cackled like teenagers.

I shook my head, a smile on my face. With all this brotherly banter and affectionate teasing, I could almost forget about Ma—the center of our universe—being sick. I'm glad we all went out after the shoot. It'd been a while since we all just kicked back and enjoyed a few drinks and laughs. Even if this place was a little…pompous for my tastes, as I preferred the laid-back, raw, earthy feeling of The Jar. Who knew, Michael might even get a professional contact out of it.

Darren and Eoin suddenly sat up, both smiling at someone over my shoulder.

Delaney must be back.

She placed down our drinks, having to bend over to the low table as she did. I rolled my eyes as Darren and Eoin's tongues nearly lolled out of their heads. She sent me a warm smile as she placed down my Jameson.

"Thanks," I said before paying her no mind. Unlike Darren and Eoin.

She was attractive, but…

Delaney looked complicated.

I guess I preferred someone more…girl next door. The kind of girl you could be best friends with.

Minutes later, I was halfway through my drink, tuning out Darren and Eoin's arguing over who was going to ask Delaney out, when Michael returned, falling into his chair with a dumbstruck look on his face like he'd been slapped.

"You struck out?" I asked. Maybe he *had* been slapped.

"You should be used to it with women," Darren said.

Eoin chuckled and gave Darren a high five.

Michael didn't react.

"You okay, Mick?" I asked him.

Michael looked at me, as if only realising where he was. "I got a meeting to pitch my business."

Damn. Good for him. "Congrats, Mick," I said raising my glass to him. "With who?"

"With…all three of them."

I whistled. This was big news for Michael.

"That was easy," Eoin said.

Yeah. A little too easy, it appeared. Michael still looked stunned.

"What did you do? Offer to sell them your soul?" joked Darren.

"Or your virginity?" added Eoin. That earned him a fist bump from Darren.

Michael shook his head. "All I had to do was—" He cut off as Delaney came by to ask if we wanted anything else.

We all shook our heads, Darren and Eoin openly drooling again, before she walked—sashayed—away.

Michael was staring at her with a strange look on his face.

"Mick?" I said.

"Huh?" He turned back to me.

I frowned. "All you had to do was what?"

Michael shook his head. "It must be nothing."

"What's nothing?" Eoin said.

"Delaney Evans," Michael said. "Our waitress. They just wanted her name."

Noah

"I thought you had plans with Prince Charming." I could only hope my dislike for Sean didn't bleed through in my voice. It still seemed surreal that Aubrey was going to marry that eejit. That she hadn't tossed him out after he ditched her on the fundraiser night.

Aubrey leaned against my truck as I pulled the noodle dish from the back seat to take into Ma's house for lunch. She glanced up at me with a slight curve at the corners of her lips. "And miss Sunday lunch with the O'Sullivans?"

"He cancelled on you, didn't he?" I was teasing, but the flash of hurt in her eyes told me I'd hit home. She stared at the ground and I slid an arm around her shoulders, knowing I needed to apologize for the dick she was with. "I'm sorry."

She lifted both shoulders slightly. "He had work."

"Well, isn't that the shit?" Darren asked, walking past us with a casserole dish in hand.

His grin told me all I needed to know about how long he'd been listening and how much he knew. I wanted to flip him a middle finger, but Aubrey beat me to it. A flash of pride buzzed through me as she shouted after him.

"I'll dump that casserole dish over your head!"

"Good luck, short stuff," Darren said over his shoulder as he stepped into the house.

Eoin scurried past us, a bag of rolls in hand. "Want me to hit him?" he asked Aubrey with a grin that made me want to hit him.

"With that?" she asked, gesturing to the rolls in his hands. But he was already gone.

A moment later I heard Darren shout something profane and my mother spoke up, her sharp voice rising over all else. "Darren Rory O'Sullivan, put your brother down right this second!"

With that, Aubrey was off like a startled deer.

I hurried to keep up. Inside the front door of the house I grew up in, I saw Darren with Eoin in a headlock, his knuckles still on Eoin's hair as he stared at Ma.

Darren huffed before releasing Eoin, who popped free and rubbed his head with a rueful look on his face. *"Worth it,"* he mouthed to Aubrey, giving her a thumbs-up as if to show he got even with Darren for her.

I repressed a growl. My little brother's grin and subsequent dimple could melt a lady's heart, and I didn't want that noise around Aubrey.

"Well, isn't it my favorite," my ma's voice called out.

I turned to my ma with a grin, arms out, ready for a hug that I knew smelled like home-baked ginger nut biscuits and lemon soap.

My ma—the traitor—walked right past me and went straight to Aubrey, pulling her into a hug.

My jaw dropped. The cheek!

Aubrey chuckled and shot me a wink over my ma's shoulder.

"It's so good to see you, Aubrey," Ma said, giving the woman I loved a sweet smile. Ma had pulled her long silver hair back loosely and her blue eyes—so like my own—seemed more tired than usual. We'd all grown taller than her by about eleven years old. Despite our wild ways, we were always respectful and loving with her even when we wanted to kill each other.

"And you," Aubrey said. Her features morphed into concern as she studied my ma. I wondered if Aubrey could see the slight pallor to my ma's cheeks. "How are you feeling?"

"Oh, you fuss just like the rest of them." My mother made a noise and waved away the comment. "I'm grand." She turned to me. "Come here, boy. Stop your pouting. You know you're at least my third favorite."

I leaned down for a hug, holding her shoulders gently, and inhaled the smell of home. "How are you, Ma? You feeling okay?"

My ma snorted as she pulled away. "Jaysus, boy, I'm not turned to glass. Just a poor ticker. Are you hungry?"

In minutes, we'd all sat at the table that my brothers and I had set with Aubrey's help. Sitting around the table with my ma right there, I could almost pretend nothing was wrong. That this was yet another day, like the vast catalogue of happy childhood memories I could draw from.

I never thought there would come a day when I'd have to sit here without my ma.

The thought slammed into me with full force. I had to bring my napkin to my face to hide myself. My ma would not appreciate me getting emotional at her table.

Darren spotted me, giving me a mirrored look of pain before locking on our ma's face like he had to memorize every detail, lest he forget. He was thinking all the worst like I was.

My chest filled with determination. I was going to do whatever it took to make sure we could pay for her surgery. Come hell or high water, I'd make sure she had the best chance at surviving this. This lottery would work.

Luckily, no one else spotted my near-breakdown. Everyone

else was focused on my ma as she peppered Aubrey with questions about the fundraiser.

"The boys told me what you did for me in organizing that fundraiser. My God, Aubrey, you are an absolute gem. If only one of my boys had been smart enough to snap you up before that man of yours did." Ma shot us—me especially—a stern look.

Aubrey chuckled. "I daresay that any woman who manages to pin down any of your boys would be a lucky woman."

My brothers looked chuffed.

Eoin had the nerve to send Aubrey a wink across the table.

I kicked out. I missed, obviously because it was Michael who let out a grunt and glared at me.

"Things going well with him? What was his name again?"

Aubrey flushed before nodding. "Sean. Yes. All fine."

"All fine? Sounds like a woman deeply in love." My ma sent me a weighted look.

This time I wanted to kick my ma under the table. I refrained, of course.

"I couldn't believe that you got that handsome young man, Jason Reilly, there," my ma continued.

Aubrey chuckled. "He was pretty easy to convince once I was able to get past his assistant."

"I bet he was," Eoin said, eyeing Aubrey up.

I aimed another kick, which Eoin was smart enough to avoid. He stuck out his tongue at me. I sent him a look that told him he was going to pay for it.

I rolled my eyes as my ma nattered on further about Jason fucking Reilly. "Come on, he's not *that* handsome."

My ma gasped. "Yes, he is. Don't you think, Aubrey?"

Aubrey nodded. "Incredibly handsome."

I choked on a too large mouthful of casserole. Michael took the opportunity to slap my back good and hard. I swatted his hand away and reached for the water, glaring at Eoin, who was smirking at me from across the table.

"He's not as handsome as your boys, though," Aubrey said to my ma. When my eyes shot to her, she was looking at me. She sent me a wink before turning back to her food. She thought I was handsome?

"I hope Noah thanked you properly for that fundraiser," my ma said, giving me a sideways glance.

Aubrey looked at me too, a slight smile on the corners of her lips as if she knew she had the power to ruin me right then. "Of course."

"Maybe give you a raise? Time off, something like that? Like a good boss would." Ma shot me a warning look.

"He's the best boss," Aubrey said with a smile, her quick defense of me warming my heart.

"I bet he is," Eoin said, elbowing Michael, who scooted his

chair out of reach of Eoin's jabbing elbow. The boy had some power for only being twenty-one, no doubt from his rugby training. "He works her long into the night. Gives her a long hard shift."

Darren let out a snort which he poorly disguised as a cough. Even Michael sniggered into his casserole.

Aubrey tried to ignore Eoin, but the slight pink in her cheeks told me that she heard him alright. With a well-aimed kick, I managed to make Eoin wince and say "Ow!" Of course, he knew it was me. *"It's on, asshole,"* he mouthed.

"Bring it, asswipe," I mouthed back.

"No fighting at the table, boys," Ma said, glaring at us before focusing on Aubrey again with a soft smile back on her face. I swear my ma loved Aubrey as much as I did. "And what's the news about your upcoming wedding?" Ma asked Aubrey, who shifted in her seat.

There were no plans. I knew Aubrey wasn't comfortable admitting that fact.

"Ma, stop pestering her and let her eat," I said.

Instantly, Michael's attention snapped to me.

Eoin's mouth dropped open and a bit of roll tumbled out onto his plate, earning him a glare from Ma.

Even Darren stared, his bite of food forgotten on the fork suspended halfway to his mouth.

Aubrey's expression of soft thanks made it all worth it. "We haven't planned anything," she said.

"No plans." I noticed a wicked twinkle in my ma's eyes. "Is that so?"

Aubrey nodded, pushing some noodles around her plate while Eoin and Darren got into a fight over the last roll.

"You've barely touched your food," Michael pointed out to Ma.

She looked down in surprise. "I guess you're right. Good company and so much to talk about." The excuse felt thin and I knew she didn't have an appetite. We'd brought all the food so she wouldn't have to deal with the strain of cooking for us, but seeing her not eat bothered me.

Eoin planted both elbows on the table and stared at Ma like he was never going to see her again.

"Don't give me that look," she said to him, swatting at his shoulder. "I'm not dead yet. Not going without a fight either."

Eoin choked.

Darren and I exchanged a grim look.

Michael paled and stared down at his food.

"Ma," Eoin said, his voice going all weird, sounding every bit like he did when he was ten.

"Yer alright, boys," my ma said, not meeting any of our eyes, her voice filled with warmth. "Even if I had to go tomorrow, I'd go with my chin up knowing that I raised you well."

A heavy silence descended over the table.

What if we lost our ma? I balled my hands into fists in my lap.

Eoin looked like he was about to burst, his cheeks were so red.

No one spoke—no one knew what to say as the grim blanket of doom slowly suffocated us all.

"The casserole is surprisingly good," Aubrey said, just a little too loud, directing her comment to Darren.

"You can thank *Dunnes* not Darren for that," Michael said with a smirk, referring to a local grocery store.

"Hey!" Darren punched Michael's arm. "I'll have you know I slaved for ages over that."

"It must have been hard work taking off the packaging and figuring out how to reheat it," Eoin chimed in.

Darren shot him a glare.

"Regardless…" Aubrey gathered a large bit of casserole on her fork. "I'm glad I didn't dump this over your head, Darren."

Darren waved his fork at Aubrey, the hint of a smile on his lips. "The moment Noah's back is turned, short stuff…" Darren let his threat hang.

"Yeah, the moment Noah's back is turned…" Eoin waggled his eyebrows suggestively.

Aaaaand we were back to normal. Or at least, as normal as the O'Sullivan household got, the fog having been lifted. At least for now.

I caught Aubrey's eye and grabbed her hand under the table. I mouthed, *thank you.*

She laced her fingers with mine. And shrugged as if to say, *that's what friends are for.*

I could have sat there for the rest of dinner just holding her hand, her tiny delicate fingers interlaced with mine.

A phone ringing cut into the noise of my brothers throwing digs at each other across the table. Aubrey pulled her hand from me and I cursed whoever was calling.

"Sorry, I meant to turn it off." Aubrey turned a few shades of pink before pulling out her cell. She silenced the phone and shoved it back into her purse. It started to ring again. She fumbled around and the noise cut off. "Sorry, it's Sean."

I flinched at his name and tore apart the roll on my plate, hoping it wasn't obvious to anyone else that I disliked him.

Her phone rang for a third time and I repressed a growl. What the feck was his problem?

"You should answer it, love," my ma said softly.

"Sorry." Aubrey chewed her lip. "He probably won't stop calling until I pick up."

"Go, go," Ma said, waving her out of the room.

Aubrey rose from her chair and hurried out.

The second she was gone all eyes were on me.

"What?" I asked.

My ma—my usually civilized ma—snorted. "You're a bloody eejit, Noah O'Sullivan. You should have snatched her up when you had the chance."

Noah

Eoin sat down on the mechanic's creeper that Darren used to lie back and roll under vehicles to work on them, a disgusted look on his face. It was a few days later and we were all at Darren's shop after hours to go through the photos from the lottery shoot. The guys were struggling for seating because everything was covered in a layer of dirt, grime or grease. Or some mixture of all three.

Michael refused to sit down at all; instead, he brushed his hands over his suit like he was going to become soiled simply by association. "Everything's so dirty," he said, curling his lip a little. "When was the last time you cleaned this place?"

"No wonder you're always filthy," Eoin said to Darren.

I sat right down next to Darren, and he gave me a look of relief like I'd backed him up somehow with this gesture. The truth was that I didn't give a damn if my torn jeans or old tee shirt got dirty. I worked in a damn bar. I'd had puke on me more times than I could count, blood from breaking up fights, and even shit once—but that was a story for another time. Grease or dirt were of no concern to me.

"Go feck yourselves, then," Darren said, motioning them both towards the door. "I'll get this site up and running without you pricks and pick the worst image of both you bastards."

Instantly, Michael came closer and Eoin sat up a bit, using his legs to crab walk the creeper closer so he could have a look.

Darren pulled the images up on the screen, and we began to cycle through them one by one. Since the plan was for all four of us to be part of this, we'd all been included in the images. Of course, we'd included wordage that told contestants they could pick one of us, two of us, or any combination they preferred, should they win.

All of us leaned in and studied the images like our lives depended on it. The four of us had posed for some shots in only our jeans and masks. Some were candid, a few featured Eoin taking a hook to the face for playfully slapping Michael's ass and telling him how well his jeans fit. I don't think I've ever seen Michael deck someone so fast, and it was the first time I'd had a bit of concern. What if the guys actually had to share a woman? Would they be able to do so?

"The masks make us look weird," Eoin said, breaking the tense silence.

I had to agree with him. Maybe because I'd never seen us like this. We'd each gone with simple green masks that were readily available and simple enough not to be easily traced back to us specifically.

Still, we could be a bunch of strangers. I recognized myself in the lineup, and there were clues, like their green eyes and my blue eyes, but nobody could figure us out based on just our eye color alone, right? Nobody knew us *that* well.

"Nobody will figure it out, right?"

I could tell that Eoin was having the same thoughts I was.

"I don't give a damn," Darren said. "I'd do anything for Ma."

I nodded, as did Michael.

Eoin chimed in with an enthusiastic, "Hell yeah!"

"So long as everyone does their part, it'll all be fine." Darren was focused on the images as he clicked through the digital copies.

"I did mine," Eoin said. "That photographer got some good shots."

I hadn't seen anything amazing yet, but I agreed. They were good shots. Some part of me was holding off from an *ah-ha, that's the one* moment and another part of me was secretly filing away second choices in case no *ah-ha* moment came.

"I've got the NDA drafted," Michael said, glancing from me to Darren. "Clearly, Darren's got the tech wizardry going on." He clapped our brother on the back, then pulled his hand away and stared at it, horrified at the grease and filth now smudged on his hand.

"I'm still not sure anyone's even going to go for this," Eoin said, settling back and crossing his arms. "Anyone will fuck a chick. Especially a hot rich chick. Why would one go for us?"

"Besides the obvious fact that we're Irish, tall, and good-looking?" Michael asked, discreetly wiping his hand on Darren's chair. His hand came away dirtier than before and he made a face, clearly regretting it.

Darren shot the lounging Eoin a glare. "We put in too much work for you to back out now."

I watched, wishing I had popcorn to enjoy while the idiots got into a row.

Eoin lifted both hands. "I wasn't saying I give up," he was quick to clarify, "just that you're all a bunch of ugly fuckers no sane woman would want inside her." He did a fist pump.

Michael pressed his fingertips into his temple before ripping his hand away from his face and staring at it in horror.

"Use the damn orange cleaner and wash your hands, Michael," Darren said, turning around.

Michael found the orange bottle and depressed the pump a good ten times in his hand, then hurried off to the bathroom to wash his hands.

"That's been bothering him for a while now," I said with a chuckle.

"I know," Darren said, a wide grin spreading across his face. "I knew he'd touch my shoulder. I might have accidentally left a glob of grease there earlier."

"Fecking evil," Eoin said, scooting the creeper closer. "I love it."

"That's because you're not the target," Michael said dryly, coming out of the bathroom with clean hands.

Eoin flipped him the bird.

Michael walked over and planted a foot on the creeper before giving it a shove that sent Eoin sailing across the room into the wall. I went back to looking at images with Darren, ignoring the spat between Michael and Eoin.

Three pictures later and one popped up that hit me with an electric tingle that set the hairs on my arm straight up.

"That's the one," I said.

Eoin and Michael went quiet, then scrambled over to look at the picture Darren had stopped on.

All of our attention fixed on the image even though I heard Eoin smack Michael in the back of the head and scoot out of reach.

In the image Eoin was to the left, leaning back a bit, his abs flexed and his arms crossed tightly. He looked every bit like the rugby champ he was, while no one would have a clue it was him.

Michael was to the right and back a little bit with his chin tilted up, his stance upright. Somehow the image captured his uppity air and gave him that rich appearance he'd worked so hard for, but not in a bad, dickish way.

Darren, to the far right, had hunched forward, his arms flexed in a rounded shape just below the belt, showing off the power in his shoulders and arms. I could see his mouth was open in a roar under the green mask.

I stood in the middle, chin up, hands spread in a "come at me" gesture. There was a primal air to us and I knew without a doubt that this was the one. This was the panty dropper. This was the one that would make the ladies beg us to fulfil their darkest, deepest, and most perverted fantasies.

"All agreed on this one?" Darren asked, glancing at all of us.

Michael nodded, speechless for once.

"I look feckin' hot," Eoin said, giving a harsh nod. "Agreed."

"This is the one, then," Darren said, hesitating a second like he was waiting for anyone to voice some concern or second thoughts.

I held my breath, ready to sucker punch anyone who had second thoughts square in the gut.

Nobody said a word.

Darren dragged and dropped the image in place.

The second he let go, I felt the collective intake of air around me. We were all kind of dreading this to some degree, I think.

Except Eoin, who seemed unfazed as he carefully worked Michael's wallet out of his pocket the last little bit. The little feckin' sneak. I hadn't even seen him working on it, but I saw it slip free. Eoin froze, then placed a finger over his lips in a plea for my silence. I shook my head in refusal and he opened the wallet wide like he was offering to bribe me with Michael's money to keep my mouth shut.

I pulled out my wallet, hoping the fucker hadn't hit me first. When I was satisfied everything was in place, I glanced up and caught the odd look on Michael's face, Darren's lifted brows, and Eoin's grin.

I put my wallet back, wedging it far down and shifting onto it so the rat bastard couldn't get it from me.

"How are we going to pick a winner?" Michael asked. "Are we just going to choose one?"

Darren shook his head. "I've installed a giveaway plugin that will pick a winner at random when the countdown ends. It'll send out a winner's email automatically. Once they've confirmed their prize, it'll send them the NDA to sign."

I chuckled. "You're going with a high-tech version of what I was thinking. I was just going to *pin the tail on the donkey* that shit."

"A child's game and the word 'shit' should never share a sentence," Darren said.

Something dark crossed my mind. "What if the fantasy is…I don't know, illegal or something?" I asked.

"The giveaway will flag any dangerous, illegal, and degrading entries using a keyword scanner and remove them from the draw," Darren said.

"I've already included a clause in the lottery terms and conditions stating that fact," interjected Michael.

"Too smart," Eoin muttered under his breath.

"Is everything else set up?" Michael asked.

Everyone glanced sideways at me.

I had been the one they'd picked to manage the whole thing. I nodded. "We're good to go."

"Okay, I'm making the website public...now." Darren leaned back in his chair, still staring at the computer screen like he wished he could take it all back. "We're live, boys."

"So what now?" Eoin sounded unsure.

"Now, we wait."

Eoin groaned.

The lottery had thirty days to run. Thirty days of counting entries, counting cash and praying we earned enough to pay for Ma's surgery.

Something told me that waiting would prove to be the worst part of all.

Lottery Entry #1

Let me just clarify, I'm a normal woman. A wife. A mom. I do school runs and cut crusts off my children's sandwiches. I wear beige and sensible shoes.

But I've always fantasied about being a stripper.

I want to take off my clothes in a private lap dance for one of you. To slowly reveal my body just for your eyes, to grind on your lap where I can feel you getting rock hard.

And when you reach for me with one hand and pull out your thick cock with the other, I shouldn't let you. It's against the rules. But I'm too horny, too wet, too needy to push you away. I let you grip my hips and slide me down on your cock, where I keep grinding to the music, our mouths slammed against each other to stop us from making noise and alerting the bouncer standing just outside the private room door.

Noah

It was a *pitiful* amount of entries.

I sat back from my computer with a sigh and grabbed my open beer from the desk, glaring at the entries that were waiting to be read.

It was already two days in and only a handful. Just a few. Not nearly as many as we'd hoped and absolutely not enough to help this growing sense of dread I had that this idea wasn't going to work.

This wasn't going to work. We were going to have to find another way. Something else. I could sell the bar.

My attention went back to the screen. I would give this a go, give it my all first. Then if worse came to worst, I'd sell the damn bar and try to get enough for it that I could cover Ma's surgery. Then I'd be out trying to find a job or begging the new owner to let me stay on. And not just myself, but Aubrey too. With her expired visa there were just no other opportunities for her. She'd be out on her ass and quickly without me being willing to bend the rules and pay her cash in hand. No, I needed to figure out how to make this work.

I knew what the problem was. No visibility. We needed to think of a way to get this out there. We needed it to go viral.

But how?

It was even harder to do since we were not able to attach our names to it. I mean, it's not like Eoin could use his rising star status in rugby to promote us, and Michael wasn't about to pitch it to his rich friends. Darren wasn't going to hang fliers about it in his shop windows; not that we'd find the right kind of attention there, either.

We'd pushed it a bit on social media with a dummy account that Darren had created, but it was going stagnant, not getting any traction. We needed it picked up by someone big. Or by some news outlet. If only we could give the reason we were trying to raise money, that heartstring tug might push people to give it a go; but that would give us away.

I didn't want pity anyway. I wanted to make my mother well.

I took a deep drink of my Guinness and sat, feeling utterly alone. The bar had been quiet on Aubrey's days off and I was missing her terribly. I hated having this secret from her; I hated the sneaking around, but I couldn't very well tell her the truth, now could I?

I stared at the entries, taking another gulp of my beer. What would she say if she knew? Would she be able to justify it the same way I was—that it was okay to do whatever it took to save my mother's life?

With the way this whole idea seemed to be fizzling out, did any of it even matter?

Aubrey

Fridays at The Jar were usually packed. This Friday we were hosting an open mike night to celebrate the end of term for the Dublin College of Music. Noah had agreed to let Danny O'Donaghue—rising star, indie rock god and guest college professor—bring his students in for a graded performance. Word had obviously spread because the bar was jammed.

Even I wasn't immune to the rush that filled the space. Or the way that the whole room seemed to be focused on the corner where Danny now sat near the stage, watching as his students performed one by one. I was half listening to the music as I served thirsty students, my hip shaking along to some of the more upbeat songs.

They were all good; you had to be good to even get into the Dublin College of Music—but there definitely seemed to be some students who stood out from the rest. Some that made my gaze move past the shoulder of the patron in front of me to the stage. Some that made the patrons forget about their drinks for a second.

I spotted a familiar figure leaning against a wall. Noah. He had his back to me, but I'd recognize his wide frame anywhere.

"Oh my God, amiga," Candace said from my side. "Do you think he'd sign my shirt?"

"Who, Noah?" I asked, totally confused. I tore my eyes away from him and found Candace giving me a knowing look.

"No, Danny."

My cheeks heated. Danny. Right. "I don't know. Doesn't hurt to ask, right?"

"I loved his songs when he played with The Untouchables, but I *looooved* his first solo single, you know what I mean?"

"Sure," I said. I was distracted by the sight of Danny slipping through the crowd to greet Noah with a hug and a back slap.

Standing there together, I could almost hear the sound of panties dropping. These two boys were like chalk and cheese: Noah with his classic golden-boy good looks, a fitted blue tee and faded denim; Danny with his midnight hair and broody eyes in dark jeans ripped at the knees, a fitted black shirt over his muscled body, a studded leather cuff around his left wrist. Noah laughed at something Danny said and my stomach tightened. Noah had been distant lately, his laughs not coming as freely with me as usual. I almost felt like he'd been avoiding me. I couldn't figure out why.

As if Noah could hear my thoughts, he turned right at that moment and caught my eye.

Shit. Busted staring. I gave him a weak smile.

Noah grinned and waved me over. I held up two fingers to indicate to give me a minute. "Can you hold the fort for a second, Candi?"

Candace squealed beside me. "Nossa, amiga, Danny is so freaking hot, get his number and have his babies for me pleeeeease."

I laughed her off, wiping my hands on the cloth tucked into the back of my shorts. "I have a boyfriend, Candace," I said. "What would I be doing with Danny's number?"

Candace gave me an exasperated look. "Giving it to me, *obviously*."

I ducked under the bar and squeezed through the crowd until I got to Noah's side.

"Aubrey, I'd like you to meet Danny." Noah leaned into my ear as if he was telling me a secret. "Don't tell anyone, but he's not as much of an asshole as he makes out to be."

"Don't say that. She might actually *like* me," Danny said with a wry smile. His voice was every bit as deep and husky as in his songs.

Noah laughed. "I'm sure you'd just say something rude enough to keep that from happening."

"In that case," I said, "I'm offended to meet you, Danny." I shook his hand, his grip firm and warm, his eyes never once blinking, but there was the touch of amusement at his lips. I could feel the star power rolling off him. I wasn't a fan, not like Candace was, but even I was feeling a little flustered under his stare.

"You keeping this boy out of trouble?" Danny said to me, indicating Noah.

Noah laughed by my side. "*She* is the one who gets *me* into trouble." He slung an arm around my shoulders. Just like that, the weirdness and distance was gone between us. I leaned into Noah, enjoying his nearness.

"Your students all sound good," I said to Danny. "Really good." I nodded up at the stage where two guys were performing.

Danny shrugged, his eyes darting to the stage behind him. "They're mostly generic, bland and unoriginal. Some of them are alright, I guess."

Wow, tough critic.

"And it took all of fifteen seconds before the first asshole comment." Noah tapped at his wrist. "Must be a record, Danny."

"Any stars in the midst?" I asked, trying to keep the tone light.

Danny's jaw tightened and something flashed behind his eyes. "No."

Al-righty then.

Noah laughed. "Jaysus, Danny. They can't be that bad." Noah turned to me. "Danny's hamming it up in order to protect his broody rock star rep."

Danny shot Noah a smirk but I could see the affection there.

I sensed something more going on beneath Danny's complicated façade. I shook off the curiosity. Complicated men weren't my thing. No matter how gorgeous they were.

I liked simple men. Not simple-minded men, but ones with good morals, clear values. The boy-next-door kind of guy. Someone I could be…best friends with. Noah's arm suddenly felt heavy on my shoulder.

"Well," I said, stepping out from Noah's arm, "I should get back to the bar before the customers revolt." I turned towards the rock star and was caught once more under his icy blue stare. "Nice to meet you, Danny." To my horror, I curtseyed. Curtseyed. What an idiot.

I could almost hear Danny and Noah chuckling at me as I hightailed it back to the bar.

Noah

I watched as Aubrey squeezed her tiny frame back through the crowd to the bar. I wanted to go with her, to clear a path before her, but I remained frozen where I stood.

"You like her," Danny said, snapping me out of my reverie.

"What? No," I protested.

Danny let out a snort. "Don't try and trick a trickster. I can spot those hazy, goo-eyes when you look at her when she's not watching. You know your body follows her throughout the room?"

"It does not!" *Does it?*

I was used to being ribbed by my family about Aubrey, but Danny…he and I were good mates, but we hadn't seen each other in months because he'd been overseas touring and living in London. If he could spot my feelings for Aubrey in less than ten minutes…who else could?

"Don't look so feckin' panicked," Danny said, clasping a hand on my shoulder. "I'm not going to go spill your secret."

"I didn't think it was that obvious," I admitted, my shoulders slumping.

"It's not. But I make a career writing songs about unrequited love. I…I know it when I see it." His eyes flashed to the stage where one of his students, a strawberry-brown-haired willowy creature was setting up with another male student. Something passed across his features.

Oh.

Oh.

"Who is she?" I asked softly.

He let out a long sigh. "Nobody." He looked back at me, his guard back up across his face. "Just a student."

A teacher in love with his student. Yikes. That was a heartbreak waiting to happen.

"I've got to get back. I'm supposed to be marking them,"

Danny said, his gaze drawing back to the girl on the stage. "I'll tweet about your lottery, no bother. I won't mention you."

I let out a sigh of relief. "Thanks, Danny."

"You feckin' owe me though, you dirty bastard," he said with a tiny smile pulling at the corner of his lip.

I grinned at him. "Whatever you need, Danny."

He clasped me in a one-shouldered bro hug before moving back across the crowded bar, people around him parting like he was Moses.

Most people were jealous of Danny—of his fame, his talent, his piles of money. None of those things really mattered to me. Maybe that's why Danny and I became fast friends after he played his first gig here. I treated him like a normal human being, instead of the rising star that he was.

Call me simple, but I just wanted to run my bar and spend time with the people I loved. I found my gaze slipping over to where Aubrey was serving customers. She tucked a stray strand of hair behind her ears and laughed at something Candace said. My stomach flipped. It didn't matter how many times I looked at her, she still caused that reaction in me.

It would all change soon though. Soon she'd be married to another man. She'd get a job working somewhere else. She'd move on with her life. Aubrey was smart and clever and could do so much more with herself than work a bar. The truth was, the life I offered was too simple for her. It wasn't good enough. Maybe that's why I never made a move on her. I knew that one day she'd outgrow this place.

And me.

Until she did, I'd hang on for dear life. Even if I only ever got to be *just* her friend.

Noah

Danny: **It's done. Good luck.**

"Text from a girl?" Aubrey asked.

I looked up from my phone. "No, why would you think that?"

Aubrey and I were the last ones in the bar closing up.

Tonight's open mike night had been more packed than usual, not surprisingly as Danny was in the house, so cleanup was taking longer than normal.

Aubrey gave me a pointed look. "Because of the shit-eating grin that you just got."

"It's just Danny with some good news," I said. The last thing I wanted was Aubrey thinking I was messaging some girl.

"Oh?" she asked, slowly creeping closer to me.

"Don't even think about it." I locked my phone and shoved it into my back pocket so she couldn't steal it and read through Danny's message. Not that she'd get any information out of it even if she did. Danny's message gave nothing away.

Aubrey placed a hand on her jutted hip and pouted, telling me that she had been thinking of doing exactly that. I knew her too well. "You're being very cagey, Mr. O'Sullivan."

I laughed. I loved it when she gave me sass. "You're being very nosy, Ms. Campbell."

"I'm your best friend. I deserve to know everything."

Guilt threaded through me. My one secret had turned into two. She deserved to know what we were doing with the lottery. She deserved to know that I'd been in love with her for years. I should confess everything to her now. Lay all my cards out on the table before it was too late. All the words I'd never said to her jammed in my throat, making it feel like it was closing up.

I shoved all those thoughts down and forced a smirk to my face. "Is that so?"

Aubrey's eyes narrowed and she waggled a finger at me. "Don't make me tickle it out of you."

I laughed, pushing her hand away. "Relax. He just did me a favor, that's all." I shot her a pleading look, like *please, let this go.*

Aubrey let out a sigh. "Alright, alright. Bro-code. Boys only. I get it."

My shoulders sagged with relief.

A strange look crossed Aubrey's face. She let out a sigh and turned back to wipe at the bar with her cloth. "That's so cool that you and Danny are friends." Her voice had suddenly gone all breathy and up an octave.

I raised an eyebrow at her. "What is that?"

"What's what?"

"We always get musos in here. You've never reacted like *that.*" I pointed a finger and circled it around at her.

She shrugged, but I swear her cheeks had gone a shade of pink.

"You think Danny's hot?" I asked, my voice coming out tight.

She shrugged again. "Maybe."

"You're taken, Rey," I bit out. Why do I want to punch Danny in the face right now? Even after he'd done me a favor and tweeted about the lottery?

Aubrey giggled. "Naw. It's so cute that you're getting jealous on Sean's behalf."

Yeah, sure. I was jealous on *that feckin' eejit's* behalf. I obviously wasn't doing a very good job of schooling my emotions because she could read me like a book. But then again, Aubrey has always been able to read me, she seemed to know when things were wrong, what I wanted, what I needed.

Except…when it came to her.

I turned towards the rack of freshly dishwashed pint glasses I was putting away and glared at them instead of her. "Yeah, well. I think Danny is in love with someone else, so…you're out of luck."

"The pretty girl who sang the 'Sorry' duet."

My gaze snapped to her.

"I'm right, aren't I?"

I blinked. How did she…?

She nodded knowingly as if I'd answered.

A realization struck me. "Did you overhear us?" Oh, shit. Did she hear Danny and me talking about the lottery? About my feelings for her?

Aubrey raised an eyebrow. "I could see the way he was looking at her."

Right. Right. Aubrey was a perceptive girl. She always had been. Except when it came to herself. She couldn't see that Sean wasn't right for her. That he didn't really love her. She couldn't see what was right in front of her.

Me.

Lottery Entry #279

I've never told anyone this. I can't imagine what people would say if they knew. I mean, I'm a freak, right? Anyway, it's not like you can judge. Thank God for the NDA. No one would ever know except for us…

I want the four of you to "break in" to my apartment and take me by force. To have you hold me down, tear clothes off me, press my face into the mattress and one by one have your wicked, wicked way with me, over and over until I'm a liquid mess.

"Thank you for taking me home." Aubrey sounded a bit off from the passenger seat of my truck, but I couldn't quite place it. "You sure you don't want to come hang out?"

I did. Of course I did. I hated parting from Aubrey. But I was bad company lately, tonight especially because my mind was on this lottery. I was undeniably preoccupied. I wanted to race home so I could check to see if Danny's tweet had helped any. The longer I stayed in Aubrey's company, the more my secrets churned in my belly.

I gave Aubrey a tired smile. "Sorry, Rey. I'm so exhausted I'd be shite company. I'd be no craic at all. And I have a load of admin crap I have to get done before tomorrow's shift."

"Oh, okay."

"I'll wait for you to get up and turn on your light," I said, giving her a smile I didn't really feel before letting it die off my lips. There was no need for pretense. She'd know better and wouldn't appreciate it.

Aubrey climbed out, but instead of closing the door, she stuck her head back in. Her shiny dark hair fell forward around her face and the scent of her tropical coconut shampoo wafted over me.

"I've missed you, you know?" she said.

I stared at her, surprised. "You took the thought right out of my head," I said. It might not be true right this second, but I've thought it since I'd started this little project. I'd been distant. Preoccupied. Sometimes, downright avoiding her. For good reason. "Let's get together soon and catch up, okay?"

She nodded at my suggestion, suppressing a yawn. "That sounds good. Drive safely and text me when you get in, okay?"

She sounded so sleepy I wanted nothing more than to carry her into her apartment, place her onto her bed—

That was not an option.

"Good night, Rey," I said instead.

She nodded, ending her yawn and saying, "You too." With a

gentle push, she closed the door behind her and almost tripped over the curb walking up to her building. She shot me an embarrassed grin and laughed at herself.

I shook my head slowly, lifting my hand to cover my eyes and chuckled. This woman, man. She was so damn cute. No matter how bad I was feeling, she always managed to cheer me up, even by accident.

I lowered my hand so I could watch to make sure she got into her building safely. I felt the smile die on my lips. What the fuck was I going to do when she married that eejit she was engaged to?

I doubted he'd be okay with her friendship with me. It had actually surprised me that he hadn't already told her to quit seeing me. Any man should know to worry about a guy like me spending time with his girl.

Shoving the thoughts out of my head, I watched the curtain over her window, waiting patiently for that silent bit of communication that told me she'd made it in safe and sound.

The light flashed on and off in the space of a moment—her sign that she was inside safely—and I sighed with relief. I'd told her never to walk up with her phone out, but to instead focus on her surroundings with every bit of her senses, just in case.

It had occurred to me to walk her up every time. Every time, I forced myself to stay in the car because I knew that there was a damn good chance I'd kiss her at her door.

Aubrey was my friend. Not my girlfriend. My best friend. Who happened to be engaged to another man. She deserved *not* to be kissed by her best friend.

Biting back a curse at my stupidity, I pulled away from the curb and drove home.

With Aubrey still on my mind, I sat before my computer and opened the tab that told me how many entries there were. When the page loaded, I almost fell off my chair. There were hundreds of entries! Hundreds. I had to refresh the page because I couldn't believe my damn eyes. Was it a glitch? Had something messed up? Was I in the right place?

It wasn't a glitch. It was real. In a short time, we'd received *hundreds of new entries*. I guess Danny sharing the damn thing was all it took to go viral.

I pulled out my phone and sent a message to the O'Sullivan brothers' group chat.

Me: Have you guys looked at the latest lottery stats?!?!

Michael: No. Some of us are trying to sleep.

Me: Then turn off your phone, doofus.

Michael: Work might call.

Me: WTF? Work calls u at 2am?

Michael: …

Darren: Holy fuck balls!

Me: Right?!

Darren: This just might work.

Darren's hopeful message echoed my own thoughts. This was it, the golden ticket that would help us get Ma's surgery and keep her on this great Earth for a long time coming.

Eoin: Holy shit. Some of these fantasies are…

Darren: Disgusting?

Eoin: HOT!

Darren: *eye roll* Trust u to think so.

Eoin: Hey so, these poor ladies who don't win…can I get a few of their numbers?

Me/Darren/Michael: NO!

Aubrey

"Mm, mm, *mm!*" Candace said, holding her phone to her chest and rolling her eyes heavenward. The bar was mostly quiet but the few patrons were either watching her intently or ignoring us both. I knew the guys generally had a serious hard-on for her, but I'm pretty sure she was oblivious. Or maybe she just didn't care. She wasn't the type of woman to base her self-value on what other people thought, and I loved that about her.

"Lemme guess," I said, crossing my arms and giving her a

once-over like I could read her mind in her stance. Her eyes were dancing with mischief. "You found the future Mr. Right?"

"I wish," she said. With a few steps towards me, she bent over the bar. A few appreciative male groans tempered the air, but she didn't seem to notice. I focused on her phone as she turned it around. It wasn't a dating app like I expected, but a website I'd never seen showing an image of four shirtless, muscled guys in green masks. Was it a wrestling team or something?

"Okay. So who are they?" I asked.

Candace rolled her eyes. "Duh. No one knows. That's what makes it so exciting!"

We paused as I stopped to smile and wave at a couple of regulars who came here to hide in a corner and watch one of the many TVs around the bar. They nodded at me.

Candace, both elbows still on the bar, gave them a cheeky grin. "Don't mind us," she said cheerfully.

A few of the guys who had been watching us seemed to freeze like they thought they were being called out. When they realized they were off the hook, they quickly shifted their attention away from us.

"I still don't get it," I said to Candace.

"You mean you haven't heard about the Irish Lottery?" Candace asked, both of her sharp, perfect eyebrows rising in surprise as she spoke.

"Like EuroMillions?" I asked.

Candace gave a honeyed laugh. "So *not* like the EuroMillions." She leaned in. "There are these…" she shook her phone to indicate the four men on the website, "…four hot Irishmen who are selling lottery tickets. The catch is that the prize isn't money; it's *them*."

"Like…" I lowered my voice and scanned around to make sure no one was close enough to overhear. "*Sexually?*"

She nodded, her eyes shining brightly. "I mean, maybe you could get them to clean your place shirtless or something. Scrub some clothes on those washboard abs. Who knows? But I tell you, amiga—"

"What are you guys up to?" Noah's voice cut into our talk. My cheeks instantly felt sunburned as I glanced up at him.

"Have you heard about the Irish Lottery?" Candace asked him.

I saw his throat bob as he swallowed. "Yeah, Candace and I play every week, hoping we'll win millions. No luck so far." He gave me a quick smile that did something to my stomach.

Candace laughed. "*Boring!* Not that lottery…this one," she said, showing him her phone. While she explained it to him, I studied the image on the sly.

The other three were good looking too, with green eyes and strong builds, but the one I was really drawn to was the one who looked like the ringleader, the one in the middle with blue eyes. His arms were spread in a gesture that could be threatening…or comforting. His powerful body would make any good girl squirm and the bad girls drop their panties.

"I wonder why they're doing it," I said. All the usual culprits came to mind: money, fame, sex.

"Who knows?" Noah said, moving towards a patron and popping the top off a beer before moving in our direction again. "Are you going to enter?"

"I already did," Candace said with a wide smile. "To enter, you have to tell them your fantasy. In detail."

Tell someone my fantasy? I flushed as I considered what it was that I wanted sexually. Sean and my sex life were...okay, I guess. Sometimes I felt like we were just going through the motions. I'd tried to suggest some more...*experimentation* in the bedroom with Sean earlier on in our relationship—even something as basic as for him to go down on me—but he got so embarrassed and angry that I stopped trying. There was still a lot of Catholic guilt and sexual repression sown into the culture of this country thanks to their history.

Noah was studying me. That boy could damn near read my thoughts at times. I covered my curiosity with a quick smile at Candace. "Do we even want to know what your entry was?"

Candace straightened, a grin on her face. "It was—"

"No," I yelped, covering my ears. "I don't want to know, la la la." That girl really had no boundaries.

She laughed, pulling my hands off my ears. "Relax, amiga. Your sensitive little soul is safe."

"Maybe *I* want to know," said Noah teasingly.

I shot him a glare before I could stop myself.

Candace looked between Noah and me before waggling her eyebrows. "Let's just say…four hot Irishmen could definitely fulfil my fantasy. But it'd be better if there were five."

Five? Where would she put five—?

An image came to mind. Like a jigsaw puzzle made of flesh. Oh. Wow. Heat spread across my face up to the tips of my ears. Out of the corner of my eye, I saw Noah's amused grin.

"Oh, I'm up," Candace said as if she'd not just dropped that bomb in our laps. Tray in hand, she hurried off to a freshly vacated table. Male eyes around the bar followed her as she sashayed off to clear away the mess with that ever-present cheer and smile.

I was left alone with Noah and the sticky tension still in the air.

"Would you ever do something like that?" Noah asked.

The jigsaw puzzle image came to mind. I shook my head to clear it. "Let five men use me as a pincushion? Probably not."

"I mean, would you enter this lottery?" He leaned a hip against the bar, crossed his arms loosely, and studied me intently. "Would you tell a stranger your deepest, darkest sexual fantasy? Would you let him *fulfil* that fantasy?" His voice took on a husky, rough edge that confused me.

"Absolutely not!" I said with a snort of disdain. "I'm engaged." Still, I couldn't help the curiosity that nipped at me.

Noah straightened up with a nod of understanding. "If you weren't?"

If I was single? An odd fluttering of excitement tickled me just under my ribs. I tried to ignore it. Failed. I shrugged, trying to play it cool, even as my insides burned. "Guess we'll never know."

Noah looked like he was going to keep pushing. Thankfully, Candace returned, preventing him from doing so, and he got caught up in serving a group that walked in. I took the dishes Candace dropped off and began to load them into the dishwasher while she hurried off once more.

For the rest of the shift I could swear I felt Noah's eyes on me, his question burning in my mind.

Would I do something like that? My thoughts wandered to that blue-eyed guy with his threatening pose, my insides warming every time I did.

I couldn't lie to myself. If I wasn't engaged, I would. Without a doubt. In a heartbeat. I'd be entering right this second.

But I wasn't a cheater. I wouldn't do that to Sean or anyone. I've never stepped out in a relationship and I never would.

Even if it meant my desires would never be fulfilled.

Aubrey

Me: How are u, babe?

My text to Sean had sat there, unread, almost all day. I sat in my apartment, silently curled up in a protective ball as a knot formed in my belly. It wasn't the first time my texts had gone unanswered. It'd been happening more often lately. He'd cancelled on me the last few times we were supposed to have us time. Something was up with Sean.

Maybe it was just his work. I knew they'd been giving him more responsibility lately.

But my instincts told me that it wasn't just that. Even when we had spent time together, he'd been distracted and not as affectionate as usual.

Instinctively, I scrolled to my contacts searching for Noah's name. I wanted to talk it out with him, to get his valuable male insight. I paused before I hit the call button. Noah had enough on his plate right now with his ma's failing health and his own life. He didn't need to deal with my crap. It was probably nothing, right?

I should just go over to Sean's place and ask him what was wrong. This was definitely not a conversation for over the phone. I jumped to my feet and pulled on my shoes. Grabbing my keys, I headed out the door and locked it behind me. Sean only lived a sixteen-minute walk from my place.

On my way to Sean's, I passed the huge St Patrick's Cathedral on my left; the gorgeous 800-year-old building, with its grand Gothic architecture and landscaped gardens, almost never failed to put a smile on my face. Except for now. I found myself second-guessing myself. Was I being crazy? I mean, it was just an unanswered text. He's probably busy.

But unanswered *all day*? It's not like I was a debt collector harassing him. I was his girlfriend. No, his *fiancée*. I was well within my rights to go over there. I had a key, for God's sake. That was an open invitation to go over when I liked.

Something could have happened to him. If I was worried, I could check in with him as a concerned fiancée would do.

I tried to ignore the feeling of dread creeping over me.

"Hello?" I asked, pushing open Sean's front door to stand in the small entryway. The door had been closed and locked, both of which were good signs.

I didn't hear a response, but I could hear movement.

Sean was here.

Sean lived alone in a one-bedroom flat in a restored Victorian red-brick house in Portobello. I know. I was mad to still live in dodgy inner-city Christchurch instead of living in this quiet neighborhood near the willow-lined canal. Portobello used to be Dublin's Jerusalem quarter back at the turn of the century but had turned into an upmarket Dublin suburb, well-kept gardens lining the red-brick terraces of houses, hip corner cafes and yoga spots nestled among the residences.

I slipped my shoes off so I didn't dirty the polished walnut floors before walking through the apartment in my socks. I hadn't moved in with Sean because his place had always felt strange to me; I guess I was delaying the inevitable.

This apartment felt too heavy, too traditional, too old money. I was always terrified of staining his latte-colored leather couch or marking his mahogany coffee table with my endless cups of Lyon's tea. He and I didn't have the same sense of style.

Every time I suggested more cozy additions to this place—a rug here, a large comfy armchair, quirky cushions with dogs faces on them—it'd turn into a snippy row. Even though it was going to be *our* place.

I'd let it go. At the end of the day, the decor wasn't what was important to me. I didn't care how our future home was decorated so long as it was warm, welcoming and full of love…like Noah's home.

"Sean?" I called as I approached the room he used as a study. The door was open a half inch and I gently pushed it open. Relief flooded me as I saw him, headphones in, music faintly reaching my ears, as he studied the pile of papers before him.

Of course, he was working. The man worked like mad all the time. I admired his dedication. A dedication I didn't feel I had. Yet. I guess I was waiting to find something worth being that dedicated to. With a soft smile, I walked up to him.

His eyes met mine and his whole body jolted. He ripped the headphones out of his ears, his expression suddenly furious, and I froze.

"What are you doing here?" he asked in an even tone that didn't match the fire burning in his eyes.

Stunned, I felt my mouth open, but no words came out.

His eyes focused on me, the annoyance slowly dying in them until he seemed like Sean again.

"I was worried." I swallowed hard, still shaken by his strange response to me. "You didn't answer your texts or phone calls."

His eyes skipped across the file in front of him, the papers in his hands, the work on his desk, then swept back to me. "I'm working."

"I can see that," I said. "You didn't answer my text from this morning. I was worried."

His lips pressed into a thin line. "I don't have time to be messaging you all day, Aubrey."

"It wasn't *all day*. It was one message." Which he was rude not to get back to me, by the way.

Sean gave me a look. "And the other day? The other night?"

My eyes nearly bulged out of my head. "You're acting like I send you a hundred messages a day."

Sean let out a sigh and his eyes drifted to the papers in his hand. "I don't really have time for this, babe."

"Oh, Ok, I'll just go then."

"Great."

I spluttered. "Are you freakin' serious?"

Sean let out a groan. "Jaysus, Aubrey, is this what it's going to be like?"

I couldn't believe my ears. My cheeks were getting red hot and I was about to burst. "Sean, what the hell is going on?"

"I'm *trying* to get some work done."

"No," I said coming to stand right in front of his desk. "This, whatever is going on with you, with us, has nothing to do with work."

Sean groaned. "Do we have to do this now? I have a report due—"

I grabbed the papers in his hand and flung them down on his desk, ignoring his cry of protest. "Yes, now. What is wrong?"

"Nothing."

"Don't give me that."

Sean sank back in his chair, his arms crossed over his chest a defensive posture if I ever saw one.

I told myself to breathe. I took in a deep calming breath. Then a second one.

Sean still wasn't making eye contact. He was acting like maybe if he ignored me for long enough, I'd go away.

"What are you stressed about?" I asked in a soft voice, hoping to coax the truth from him.

"It's just…work, Aubrey. I keep telling you this."

"You go days without messaging me, you've cancelled the last few times we've organized something, and when we do spend time together, it's like you're not really there," I said, trying to keep my voice as level as possible.

"I've been busy."

"Too busy *for me*," I said. "You weren't too busy to hang out with the boys the other night. Or go to rugby training."

Sean rubbed his eyes. "I just… I just don't know."

"Don't know what?"

"I mean, I was going to give it some time, you know?"

"Know what? Give what time?" My head was starting to spin.

"It just…happened so quickly. I don't think either of us really thought it through."

"Sean…" I placed my palms down on his desk, a sinking feeling growing in me, "…what are you talking about?"

He sighed in frustration. "I didn't want to do this but…I don't think I can do this."

"What do you mean…this? Do what?"

He waved a hand between us.

My heart stopped beating in my chest. Us. He meant us.

He couldn't do…*us.*

I stumbled back, falling into the chair in front of his desk. "You don't want to marry me anymore." It was a statement, not a question. The words sounded hollow from my mouth. Because I felt hollow.

Shouldn't I be…raging?

Maybe I was in shock.

I waited for the scorned fury, the heartbreaking sadness to rise up and consume me.

"I'm sorry," he said. "I just don't think either of us is ready for this commitment."

That wasn't true.

I may have been only twenty-three, but I was ready to commit to the right man. Love didn't wait till you were ready. It came along and smacked you on your ass. And if you loved that person enough, then you wanted them to be by your side as you "got ready". You'd figure out life together. With each other. Not the other way around.

"I mean, we can stay together, just…*not* get married," Sean said.

His words stung because they sounded like a consolation prize.

"I mean," he continued, sounding like he was rambling, "I asked because you need your visa and it seemed like the right thing to do at the time. I'm sure if you looked harder, if you really wanted to, you'd find a job that would get you a visa."

I let out a snort. I had been trying. Hard. How dare he suggest otherwise.

"I'm just not ready for marriage yet. Maybe I will be…"

I stared at the man I thought I was going to marry. Sean wouldn't hold my eye, staring into his lap where he was wringing his fingers. I could see that he hated that he was doing this to me. That's why he'd been avoiding me for the last few weeks.

"Say something," he blurted out, the silence obviously getting too much for him.

"What do you want me to say?"

Sean leaned forward, his brows pressed with concern. "Are you okay?"

I paused…then nodded.

Sean let out a sigh of relief and sank back into his chair. "Cool. Okay. Thank you for taking this so well. I'm sorry."

I nodded again, unable to form words, my mind whirring. Our engagement was over. But I felt…okay.

Sean was a good guy, really. He was sweet, smart and respectful. I never had to worry about him stepping out on me. But there was just something…*missing* between us. We were…a brown coat, comfortable but totally replaceable.

We had no…fire in the soul of us. No great love that would burn hot enough to last a lifetime.

This was the truth I hadn't been willing to face until now.

I slid my key to Sean's apartment onto the desk and stood.

His eyes fixed on it and widened. "What are you doing?"

"I'm sorry, too," I said.

Sean blinked at me. "You're breaking up with me? Just because I don't want to get married?"

I shook my head. "I think you and I both know that this isn't going to work."

As I walked away, my socks padding my footsteps, I wondered if Sean would come after me. If this was the part when he came after me, fought for me, begged for me to stay. The part where we caught on fire.

As I put on my shoes, I could swear I could hear him typing.

Closing his door behind me, I sucked in a deep breath, trying to process what just happened.

Sean and I were over.

Why wasn't I feeling heartbroken? Why did I feel…*relieved?*

But on some level, I understood why.

I wanted fire. I wanted to be with someone who couldn't get enough of me, even if I was in his face *all freaking day*. I wanted to be with my soulmate. With my everyday hero.

With my best friend.

For some strange reason, Noah's face popped into my mind. I shoved that aside before I could dwell on *why*.

Aubrey

"What's going on with you?"

I glanced up into Noah's blue eyes.

He stood a few feet away, arms crossed, watching me through narrowed eyes.

I finished wiping up the tiny spill on the bar while quickly considering my response.

It hadn't even been a day since Sean and I had broken up. I'd been keeping it to myself for the time being while I processed how I was feeling. I hadn't been acting any differently, or at least I didn't think so.

"Nothing," I lied. And immediately winced. Noah could always tell when I was holding something back from him.

"Shite on, it's nothing. Spill it." He wasn't going to give up until I gave him something.

"I'm just a bit tired," I said. It was true; I hadn't slept well last night. I'd tossed and turned until about 6 a.m., trying my best to figure out what to do now and how to tell everyone. All that lost sleep and I still had no answers. "I didn't sleep well last night."

Noah moved in close like he was going to give me a hug, but instead pressed his lips to my forehead. It wasn't quite a kiss, more of just a touch.

It sent a shock of warmth through me, and I froze.

He backed off a second later and frowned down at me. "You're not running a fever. How are you feeling otherwise?"

"Did you just use your lips to check my temperature?"

He nodded. "It's how Ma used to check mine. Do you want me to drive you home?"

For some strange reason, his concern brought me almost to the brink of tears. I blinked, trying to cover the sudden moisture in my eyes. I shook my head. "I'm not sick, just..." I opened my mouth to tell him the truth, that Sean had freaked out and had called off the engagement, but something stopped the words before they could leave my lips.

I let out an awkward laugh. "Just feeling emotional for no reason." I sucked in a deep breath and struggled to compose myself.

Noah pulled me into a hug and I wrapped my arms around his neck. Clinging to him, I inhaled his warm, clean scent and heard his murmur. "I'm here if you need me."

I needed him. More than I'd ever needed anyone.

A few days later, I sat alone on my couch, a piping hot cup of tea in my hand. The mug—an oversized, heavy ceramic thing covered in butterflies—steamed, and I breathed in the scent of chamomile.

Beside me, my laptop was open and on. On the screen was the image of the four Irish men of the now infamous Irish Lottery. It might sound strange, but I swear that blue eyed one looked like he was staring right at me. Through me. He may or may not have starred in a very sexy dream last night. Or at least those blue eyes were all I could remember when I'd woken all hot and bothered in a tangle of sweaty sheets.

A national news channel had gotten hold of the story, and now everybody was talking about it. All night, that's all the patrons at the bar would talk about. I heard they'd even made the international news and women from overseas were entering. It was crazy. Would women really travel all the way to Ireland to have their fantasies fulfilled?

Wouldn't I?

I thought about my response to Noah when he'd asked me if I'd consider entering this lottery.

I'd said no because I was engaged.

Now I was single and my reason was null and void. But in the harsh light of day, staring at the actual entry form, I wasn't quite as sure. Did I have the guts to go through with it?

"There's no way I'd win," I said out loud to the silent apartment. My roommate was staying at her boyfriend's place so I had the whole night and most of tomorrow to myself.

I glanced at my laptop. Four strangers. Though the site said I could pick and choose any one of them or any combo of them. My heart began to thunder and rumble in my chest and I couldn't help but wiggle a tiny bit in my seat. Nearly spilling my Lyon's tea, I took a quick sip of the hot liquid. It stung all the way down my throat and I blinked back tears.

Ah, what the hell. I might as well give it a go.

Setting my tea down on the coffee table, I picked up my laptop. With it balanced on my crossed legs, I bought the ticket and came to the box asking for my fantasy. I chewed my lip. What did I want? I could type out something elaborate, something outrageous, something akin to Candace's four-or-five-at-once desires. But was that what I truly wanted?

My fingers hovered over the keys and I let out a sigh. I typed.

I just want someone to give me an orgasm.

Short, sweet, and incredibly pathetic. My hands shook so hard I missed the enter key and had to delete the string of backslashes I'd accidentally typed into the box when I missed the key. I held my breath and touched the enter button with a single finger like a chicken peck before I could lose my nerve and change my mind. With a squeak of excitement, I saw the loading icon.

Then my laptop went black.

"What the heck?" I asked, touching the trackpad to wake it up. Had it gone into sleep mode that quickly?

The screen didn't flicker to life, so I held down the power button. Nothing.

My laptop was dead.

"Oh, God," I whispered into the empty room as my cheeks heated up like I'd been stung by a billion angry bees. The first thing anyone would see when they fixed it was that I was entering a lottery to have four hot Irishmen give me an orgasm.

Aubrey

The knock at the door surprised me. I jumped to my feet and clicked off the TV before hurrying over and opening it a crack.

Darren's green eyes met mine through the tiny opening. He grinned. "Fix-it man, at your service."

"Did Noah send you?" I asked. I'd talked to Noah on the phone last night and mentioned that my computer had died on me. He'd offered to send Darren. I'd told him not to and that I'd go have it fixed by someone next week.

Darren nodded. "Threatened me with bodily harm if I didn't."

I was being rude as hell, keeping Darren out in the drafty hall like I was. But I also knew that if he managed to boot up my computer, the page I was on could pop up and he'd see it. I did not want Darren, and as a consequence, Noah, to find out that I entered the Irish Lottery *and* what my pathetic excuse for a fantasy was.

I just want someone to give me an orgasm.

I would die of embarrassment.

"It's okay. I can get my laptop fixed by a professional," I said.

Darren slapped a hand over his heart. "Madam, you wound me."

I smiled, trying to soften my refusal. "No offense."

"You don't think I can fix it?" Darren crossed his arms over his chest as if I'd just questioned his manliness.

"I'm sure you can. But my laptop is not your problem."

He shrugged. "It's no bother. This kind of stuff gets my mind working. I like it. At least let me look at it, I came all this way here."

"Well, I…" Dammit. I couldn't come up with a good reason to tell him no. I opened the door wide and walked back to the couch. Flopping down on it, I watched him come in and pick up my laptop off the coffee table.

"What were you doing when it died?"

I could feel my face heating up. "I, uh, was online."

He chuckled. "Oh, yeah?"

It hit me, what he must be thinking. "I wasn't watching—" my voice lowered to a humiliated whisper, "—*porn*."

"None of my business what you were doing," he said in an even, calm voice like we were discussing the weather. "Just helps give me an idea of what might be wrong."

"I had a web browser open, that's all," I said.

"One tab?" He arched an eyebrow at me.

I nodded. He opened my laptop and messed with the power button. I'd had it plugged in all night, hoping that it would be as simple as needing a charge, but no such luck.

"How's your ma?" I asked.

"You know, Ma," he said as he worked. "She's going along pretending like everything's fine, the stubborn old bat." The affection in his voice was clear. "The four of us have a roster going on so that one of us is checking in on her at least once a day." Darren paused his messing to shoot me a grin. "She doesn't know about the roster so don't tell her. Although she suspects. It's driving her crazy. *Jaysus Christ, you boys are all under me feet like mice. I get rid of one of ye and another pops up. I'm not a bloody invalid, you know?*"

I laughed at Darren's high-pitched impersonation of his mother.

He chuckled along with me and pulled out a little tool set from his pocket. He flipped my laptop over and began to unscrew the little screws holding everything together with the deft hands of someone who knew what they were doing. "I don't know if I said thank you for organizing that fundraiser."

I smiled. "You did." My shoulders slumped. "It wasn't enough though."

Darren reached out and placed a hand on my arm. "Hey. It was more than enough." His smile crinkled the corners of his lovely jade eyes. He was a beautiful man. Of course he was, being related to Noah. But his touch didn't give me that strange fluttering feeling in my belly.

He continued dismantling my laptop bit by bit, placing everything just so on the coffee table like he was making a map. "How are things with Sean?" he asked without looking up at me.

I know it was meant to be a casual question. I didn't expect the lump in my throat to appear at hearing it. I didn't want to lie. I didn't want to tell him the truth. I hadn't told anyone yet. What the heck should I say? Shifting in my seat, I tried to think of a good enough deflection. Stay vague. Then I wouldn't have to lie. "He's fine."

"Fine?"

"He's…busy with work."

Darren lifted his gaze from the guts of my laptop to fix on my face. "Oh? When was the last time you saw him?"

"A few days ago," I said slowly. When we'd broken up.

"And when will you see him next?"

Ahhhh. "I…don't…know."

Darren's eyebrows furrowed. "Is everything okay with you two?"

I shrugged. See…vague. Noncommittal. Not exactly lying.

"I didn't see him at the fundraiser," Darren said as he studied me.

It felt like all the air was escaping from my lungs. I hadn't told anyone about it and it was slowly eating me alive from the inside. I wanted to say it out loud, wanted to confide in someone. I wanted someone to tell me that I wasn't some failure of a human being because of this. I blinked back tears. Ugh.

"Aubrey?" Darren's concern was enough to make this dam burst.

"We broke up," I blurted out. Just saying it felt like a weight off my shoulders.

Darren carefully put aside his tools and faced me. "Why?"

I shrugged.

"If you don't want to talk about it—"

"I suppose I could say it was because his career was taking off and we'd stopped spending so much time together. Or that he wasn't ready for marriage, but if I'm honest with myself…" I let out a long breath, "…we weren't right for each other."

Darren squeezed my shoulder. "Sometimes the hardest thing is to be honest with ourselves. You did the right thing, short stuff." The affection in his voice was a soothing salve to my wounds. "You seem…okay with it. Sad but not heartbroken."

"And that's the weirdest thing," I admitted, "I feel bad that I'm *not* heartbroken about it. Then angry at myself that I might have gone along with a wedding to a man who I didn't love enough to be wrecked over."

"But you didn't go through with it."

"I could have."

"Trust me, even if it went that far, I think there may have been a plot twist or two that might have stopped the wedding before you got to the vows."

I blinked at Darren, trying to decipher his words. Before I could ask, he spoke. "What does Noah think?"

"I…haven't told him?" My voice went all high-pitched at the end of my sentence.

"What?" Darren stared at me, my laptop all but forgotten on the coffee table. "Why not?"

It was a good question. Why hadn't I? Something stopped me when I went to tell him the other night at work. I knew I needed him, that I wanted his support. He was my best friend in the whole world and I could trust him with anything. So why hadn't I told him?

"I tried to," I said. "I just couldn't get the words out."

I didn't want to add more to Noah's shoulders right now. His ma was sick and he was worrying about her health while struggling to raise money for her surgery. He had enough to worry about without me dumping my stupid break-up on him too.

Yes, that was it.

Still, as honest and true as this was, I couldn't help feel like there was some other reason too.

I noticed Darren was watching me carefully, a serious expression on his face that seemed to be sliding into an understanding I didn't fully grasp. "Noah needs to know."

"Please don't say anything to him," I said in a panic. "You're the only person I've told."

Darren studied me for what felt like forever. When he spoke, his words were measured. "I hate the thought of keeping this from Noah."

"I will tell him, I just need…" *courage,* "…time."

"You know you're like a sister to me."

I nodded.

"That's the only reason I'm keeping my mouth shut about this." Darren grabbed a tool off the table, pointing it at me to punctuate his words. "But I'm not lying to him. If he asks me if you two broke up, I'm saying yes."

I let out a sigh of relief. "Thank you. That's all I'm asking."

"You seem more stressed about telling Noah than you are

about the breakup."

I didn't want to admit it, but Darren was right. I was sad that it was over between Sean and me. But I knew undoubtably that we'd done the right thing. The more I thought about our relationship, the more I felt like maybe I'd dodged a bullet. We weren't a perfect match by any stretch and over the last couple days I found myself wondering if we were even a good match. The biggest emotion I felt was…relief.

"I think you might be right," I said softly.

Darren lowered his attention to the laptop in his lap.

I watched him do something with the internal parts of the laptop before he began to close it all up. The final screw went in place and he flipped it over. He powered it up and the screen flashed to life.

I held my breath, praying it didn't open up on the last website I'd been on: the Irish Lottery site.

I almost cried with relief when my laptop booted up to show my desktop, messy with icons all over it, but nothing embarrassing.

"All fixed," Darren said, setting it on the coffee table.

"Thank you so much," I said, leaning in and pulling him into a quick hug. "I set aside a few hundred euros to get it fixed." I grabbed my purse and dug through it to find the money. "Is that enough?"

"You're not paying me," he said in alarm. "You're family."

"Darren. I can't give you nothing for this. I took up your afternoon."

His eyes warmed. "Then how about a cup of coffee?"

That I could do. It wasn't enough, but it was better than nothing.

"And bickies?" I asked. "I have tea cakes."

Darren rubbed my hair, mussing it up. "Short stuff, you know how to treat a man."

From the kitchen I asked him how he liked his coffee and waited for it to brew.

"Just however you make it," he called from the other room.

I winced. "You might regret that." He didn't know it but I loved my coffee with sugar and cream. I made it strong so there was a bitter bite, but the sweet hit the tongue first and the bitter snuck up behind. I'd top it off with a pinch of cinnamon.

"I doubt it. It's impossible to mess up coffee."

"Challenge accepted! Oops! That might have been salt, not sugar." I stirred in two teaspoons of sugar and held back a giggle at the gagging noise he made. With a generous dash of milk and a pinch of cinnamon, I mixed it all in and cheerfully said, "Okay, and we're ready!"

Carefully carrying the cups and a plate of tea cakes on a tray, I set them before us on the coffee table. He was studying me intently.

"What?" I asked.

He looked like he wanted to say something, but shook his head instead. "The coffee smells amazing," he said.

"Thanks. And thank you again for fixing my laptop." I was definitely going to need it now to apply for jobs so I could stay in the country. My visa deadline was still months away. I had time. I did.

"Stop thanking me. It's not a big deal." He lifted the mug of steaming hot coffee to his lips. Then made a face. "I think you really did put salt in it."

"What?"

Darren cracked up. "Joking. It's perfect, short stuff."

While we drank our coffees, Darren told me stories of the trouble Noah would get up to as a child. He had me laughing and smiling into my coffee at the thought of Noah as a boy. I liked seeing this side of Darren. He was usually the quietest one of the boys, but get him talking and he didn't shut up.

"So, any ladies on the scene for the O'Sullivan brothers?" I asked with a waggle of my eyebrows.

Darren snorted. "Well, you know Eoin."

I rolled my eyes. "Still changing girls like he changes his jocks."

Darren make a face. "If only he changed his jocks as often as he changed girls."

"Ewww." I giggled.

"And Michael's too busy with his work for women." That sounded familiar.

"And you?"

Darren shrugged and tipped the last of his coffee into his mouth. "I...I just have bad luck with women."

My heart squeezed. I ran through the catalog of single women I knew to see whether I could set Darren up with any of them. No one felt good enough for him.

"I'm not exactly a prize," Darren continued. "I'm just a lowly mechanic."

I let out a loud gasp and slapped his shoulder. "Don't you dare say that!"

"It's true. Most women want someone with wealth potential, like Michael, or famous like Eoin."

I shook my head. "Those women don't know what they're missing out on. You deserve someone really great."

Darren looked at me with surprise before grinning sheepishly at me. "Thanks, short stuff. Although, don't tell Noah you said that. He'll murder me in my sleep. I should be off." He stood.

I stood with him and gave him a quick hug. "I'm lucky as hell to have you guys in my life."

"I'm pretty sure we're the lucky ones." He hugged me back before letting me go and looking down at me. "I do want you to think about something."

I nodded, staring up at him.

"Tell Noah about your break-up. And soon. He needs to know," he said. "Everything will work out fine."

Long after Darren had gone, I stared at the door, still wondering what he'd meant by that.

Lottery Entry #3893

Don't judge me. I married young, you see, and I didn't have time to fulfil this fantasy before I made a commitment. And my husband…well, he'd never go for it. He won't even put a finger up there; he thinks it's gross. I love him. I do. I just can't seem to get this fantasy out of my head…

I just need two of you. Two of you who are the *biggest*, if you know what I mean. One of you will lie down on his back while I straddle him, his cock in my wet pussy. And the other will be behind me, spreading my cheeks and lubing me up before easing into my virgin ass. I want to feel both of you at once.

Be fucked by both of you at once.

Noah

"Holy shite."

Darren swiveled around in his chair, looking stunned.

The time had come to pick the winner and we were all in Darren's shop, much to Michael's dismay. This time he'd been careful to touch nothing. Eoin had taken it upon himself to make sure that Michael wound up dirty, rubbing his fingers in greasy spots before affectionally clasping Michael's shoulder or ruffling his perfectly coifed hair.

"So?" Michael asked Darren. "Did the program pick the winner?"

Darren nodded slowly. He inhaled and I instinctively did the same. The sharp scent of cars and rubber hit my nose, and I swallowed back the nerves gnawing at me. Why wasn't Darren saying anything?

"Is she hot?" Eoin asked.

Michael glared at him.

"What?" Eoin said, not a trace of apology in his voice. "You were all thinking it. I'm the only one who had the balls to ask." He glanced at me for backup.

I shook my head at him. "She could be as ugly as a mule and ten times as stubborn and I wouldn't give a damn," I said. "This is for Ma, not for us." I wasn't going to lose sight of what was really going on. I wouldn't forget the real reason we were doing this. It wasn't for our pleasure or for fun—it was to make sure Ma got the surgery she needed. Nothing else mattered.

Eoin grumbled but accepted what I was saying before expectantly looking at Darren.

"So, spit it out," Michael said.

"I'm sorry, Noah." Darren refused to look at me.

A knot formed in my gut. "Sorry for what?"

"The program…" he mumbled, "…it's random. I mean, what are the chances…"

I shook my head, not understanding.

I wasn't the only one because Michael let out a frustrated noise. "For Pete's sake, just spit it out. Who won?"

Darren finally looked at me, his eyes round with apology and concern. "It's Aubrey Campbell. Aubrey won."

All eyes shifted to me. The room got so quiet I could hear my blood pressure rising. I must have heard him wrong. Aubrey was engaged to be married. She wouldn't have entered this lottery. She said she'd never even consider it because she had a fiancé.

"Need a chair?" Michael asked me, whisking one behind me like he expected me to collapse.

"Dude," Eoin said, staring at me wide-eyed.

I wanted to say something. Anything. With everyone staring at me, I felt like the whole world was coming to a halt. The blood was rushing in my ears like a turbulent ocean and something tasted metallic on my tongue. I needed for this to be a sick joke. A brotherly prank. A dream...nightmare...

I needed...air.

Without a word, I headed for the door.

"I'll go with him," Michael said.

"Let him be," I heard Darren say as the door closed behind me.

Outside, I just started walking. No destination, just me and my thoughts. They were wrong. Clearly, this was a game. One that

Darren had taken too fucking far. There was no way Aubrey won. She wouldn't cheat on Sean. She wasn't that kind of person. I was her best fucking friend; I'd know if she liked to sneak around on people.

Yes, this was a joke. A prank. A lie.

Turning sharply, I headed right back in the door of the shop.

"Fuck you," I said, walking right up to Darren and grabbing him by the collar. Lifting him up out of his chair, I saw him raise a hand to stop our brothers from coming to his aid. "She would never—"

"I swear I'm not fucking with you," he said evenly while gesturing at the computer. "Go see for yourself."

I dropped him and stepped closer to the computer.

In the giveaway widget under the heading Winner, Aubrey's name was there in bold letters, as was her email address. And her fantasy:

I just want someone to give me an orgasm.

Oh, fuck.

"This is a mistake," I muttered. "Maybe…maybe Candace entered Aubrey on her behalf. Yes, that's what happened." One call to Aubrey and I'd know that she wasn't the one who bought this ticket. I pulled my phone out of my pocket.

Eoin grabbed my arm and Michael snatched my phone.

"Give it back!" I struggled against Eoin.

"You can't call her!" Eoin said. "Then she'll know it's *us*!"

Oh fuck. I couldn't ask her about it. I couldn't tell her that I knew.

But this…*her*. She couldn't be the winner. My body heated in anger, lust or both.

"Fix it!" I snapped at Darren, shrugging Eoin off me. "Pick someone else."

Darren gave me a woeful look. "I can't. The program won't let me."

"It's a fucking program! You can make it do whatever you want! Fix this!"

This was going all wrong; like watching a plane careening into the side of a mountain, I could see it all happening and I was powerless to stop it.

"The program already sent her the email telling her she won. I can't fix it," Darren said. "I'm sorry."

I could lose my best friend over this. Even if she never found out it was me, how could I live with myself keeping such a secret from her?

A suffocating silence swelled up around me. I fought the urge to destroy something. To punch Darren in the face. To take out all three of my brothers at once. I knew it wasn't Darren's fault—anyone's fault—but I needed to blame someone.

"Well…" Eoin broke the silence, "…at least she's hot."

I charged at Eoin, yelling at him that I'd rip his head off. I thrashed against a net of strong arms as Darren and Michael caught me.

Eoin was unrepentant. "What? You know she is. You've been wanting to ride her since the day you met her."

"Don't talk about her like that."

"He's got a point," Michael said softly. He continued quickly as I turned on him. "This could be how you could show her what she's missing. Noah, she said her fantasy is to come. That's a sad damn sign of the state of her love life."

"You're her best friend," Darren said, nodding. "It should be *you* that shows her."

The fury slowly drained out of my body, replaced with dark excitement pounding through my veins.

"We'd all be there, but you and Aubrey would be the stars of the fantasy."

Little bit by little bit my brothers let me go, like they knew I was no longer a threat to Eoin's life.

I wanted this. I wanted to give Aubrey an orgasm. I wanted to please her. I knew that prick Sean was a shit boyfriend; now it was confirmed. I'd fucking break his face if I ever saw him again.

But that didn't make it okay for her to cheat on him.

"I…don't know," I said.

Could I do this? Could I not only help her cheat on her shite boyfriend, but be the one she cheated with? Could I risk our friendship like this?

"She trusts you, man. It should be you," Darren said in a low voice, clapping a hand on my shoulder.

It was more fucking complicated than that. A lot more complicated.

Or was it?

Aubrey was an adult, capable of making her own choices. I'd never push her to step out on Sean, but if she'd entered the lottery on her own... And then to win. What were the chances? It was an opportunity I couldn't pass up.

Darren was still studying me. I finally gave him a tense nod. He let out a sigh of relief. I could handle this. We were going through with it.

If Aubrey and I had been dealt a hand like this, maybe...maybe it was fate.

Aubrey

I stared at my laptop screen, refreshing my inbox for easily the tenth time. It was still there. The *RE: Irish Lottery – You're a winner!* message still sat in my inbox, unopened.

I told myself it must have been some joke. Or it was spam. One of those *We got your email now! We're selling it to everyone* spambots.

I circled the message with my mouse several times, chickening out at every pass.

Was it really possible I'd won?

Surely not. I've never won anything.

Definitely spam.

Definitely—

Oh my God, Aubrey, just open the damn thing.

I doubled clicked the message to open it, pulling my hands away before I could rapid-fire jam the escape key. It opened and my eyes jumped over the words, searching for the moment it revealed itself as a scam or spam. But instead of the words *You're a winner, please take this million euro check and cash it, then money order it back to me while keeping ten thousand out for yourself*, it all looked legit.

I'd won my fantasy to be fulfilled by four hot Irishmen.

Fuck me.

Literally.

There was a button I had to click to confirm and accept the prize.

The prize…four hot, willing men that only wanted to make my fantasy—my pitiful fantasy—of having an orgasm come true.

My heart began to beat hard. My hands wouldn't stop shaking. I kept wiping them on my jeans to get rid of the moisture.

My eyes scanned the banner over the message—another shot of the four men with their masks on. All looking like they were staring out from the screen and right through me. They were going to make me come if I let them.

I felt ready to alternately hurl and pass out. I could just...not accept it. I could ignore it. They'd move on to the next winner after fourteen days of the prize not being claimed (part of the terms and conditions). I'd never speak of this to anyone. Ever.

Forget my fantasy.

Forget them. Especially the one with the blue eyes.

But if I ignored it, I knew I'd spend the rest of my life wondering *what if*.

Yes. I was doing it! Accepting prize n—

How would Noah feel if he knew I was doing this? All my excitement fled, my hand falling away from my laptop. Would he be disappointed? Shocked? Noah had only ever known me as "relationship girl". I'd basically been in a relationship with one man the whole time he'd known me. Did Noah even *think* of me as a sexual being, with needs, desires...unfulfilled ones?

What did that matter? I was single. I wasn't doing anything wrong. Besides, Noah was my best friend. It's not like I ever judged the *God of Thunder* or rolled my eyes when notes with phone numbers on it were shoved into his hand. I should be able to tell him about the lottery. He'd fist bump me, saying something like, "Go get your bit." He'd be supportive; that's just who he was, who he'd always been.

What did I really have to lose? Not Sean—we were over. Not Noah—we were just friends. Why shouldn't I do this for myself? I rarely did anything crazy. Why deny myself this one chance to be treated and pampered and loved on by four extremely sexy men there only to fulfil my every desire?

My mouse hovered over the Accept button.

Still, I hesitated.

Why? No one had to know. I couldn't tell anyone even if I wanted to what with the NDA I'd be signing. Not that that point made me feel better. I didn't keep secrets from Noah.

Except about my breakup.

I shook my head. "Come on, Aubrey," I whispered to myself. "Take what you want. Say yes."

Yes to pleasure. Yes to orgasms. Yes to four hot Irishmen making this happen for me.

My insides turned molten at the thought, filling me with resolve.

Before I could change my mind, I clicked *Accept*.

Noah

Aubrey hadn't said more than a dozen words to me all day.

Our usual fun, playful work banter was nonexistent even though she seemed like her usual self: smiling, happy, talkative with Candace.

When Darren called me to tell me that the prize had been accepted, I still hadn't been convinced it'd been her. But when Aubrey emailed back the NDA with her all too familiar signature on it, it'd confirmed that it hadn't been a mistake. Nobody had done this on her behalf.

Aubrey had entered.

Aubrey had accepted.

I've never wanted to say something more in my life. Instead, I watched her, keeping the storm raging inside me bottled up instead of dragging her into the back room like it was a confessional and demanding her secrets. Surely she'd confide in me like she always had. I had to trust that she would. Right?

It's not like you're being very forthcoming, Noah. The only reason I fucking knew she was keeping secrets was because *I was keeping secrets from her too.* Who was the asshole here, really?

Keeping a secret wasn't on par with cheating on someone you promised to marry. At least, that's how I justified it to myself.

Maybe I didn't know Aubrey as well as I thought I did? Maybe this was fate's way of kicking me in the balls when I finally fell in love. Like someone up there was looking at me and saying, "Here's the perfect woman for you!" Only when I fell head over heels, they threw in, "Oh, yeah, except there's just this one little thing."

Aubrey was going to cheat on Sean.

No matter how I thought about it, I couldn't wrap my head around it. I still couldn't believe Aubrey was that kind of person. Even if Sean had never pleased her—a thought that drove me mad with longing to fix it—it still wasn't good enough a reason for her to do the dirt.

You're about to help her cheat. What does that say about you, Noah? Despite my morals, my conscious belief that this was wrong, my heart raced and cock stiffened imagining Aubrey spreading herself out naked for me.

Aubrey tossed her head back, laughing at something—likely outrageous—Candace had said. Eyes from around the bar slid towards her. That infectious laughter drew everyone in, including me. Especially me.

A sudden possessiveness came over me. I wanted to yell at everyone to stop fucking looking at her. Almost the whole time I'd known her she'd been "taken." Part of me believed that Sean was just…holding onto Aubrey until it was my turn.

But now that I knew she'd accepted a night with four *strangers,* things were different. Would she sleep with him—that young lad paying more attention to Aubrey than the game of pool with his friends? Would she let him touch her—that businessman eating by himself who eyed her hungrily as he chewed his burger? Would she come for him—?

I heard a bang and realized that I'd slammed my fist into the countertop. Goddamn. I was making myself crazy.

Aubrey's dark-chocolate eyes met mine, her laughter gone. In its place, a look of surprise. Her furrows drew to concern. *"Are you okay?"* she mouthed.

"Grand," I mouthed back. Just fucking grand.

At the end of the night, Aubrey and I were the last two left as usual, closing in silence. No music on. No dancing with brooms or hip bumps. No fucking limes in the fucking coconuts. I guess both of us were trying to come to terms with the secrets we were keeping.

"You're awfully quiet tonight," she said in a low tone that caught my attention.

Had her voice always been this husky?

I glanced over to her.

She was watching me through her eyelashes, her chin down.

I just want an orgasm.

All I could imagine was her speaking those words to me in that voice.

Give me an orgasm, Noah.

Begging me as she stared at me through her lashes.

Make me come.

Fuck. My cock swelled to near painful. I tore my eyes away, turning my body so she wouldn't see my reaction to her. It didn't matter what I consciously thought about the matter, the voice of morality that echoed in my head, I was going to give Aubrey the night of her fucking life. I was going to make her come over and over until she forgot Sean's name. And I was going to hate myself—and her—for it.

"Stuff on my mind," I said. *Like you coming apart around my cock behind your fiancé's back.*

"Do you want to talk about—?"

"No!" I didn't mean for my tone to sound so harsh. I softened at the flash of rejection in her eyes. "Sorry. Didn't mean to snap. I just…" *Can't stop thinking about how sweet your guilty pussy will taste.*

Aubrey surprised me with a quick hug. Her smell of coconuts and vanilla washed over me, calming my whirlpool of thoughts. Faith settled over me. Aubrey wasn't a cheater. She wouldn't go through with it, I was sure.

Aubrey backed off before I could hug her back. "Your ma. I know. I can't even imagine what you're going through." She gave me a sad smile before turning away to finish up closing.

When we were done, we stepped out into the early morning air and I locked up behind us. Our breath hung in the air like ghosts, a chill nipping at my fingers as I tugged my jacket close.

"Confession time?" Aubrey said.

My heart rate leapt into overdrive.

Was she about to tell me the truth? Was she going to tell me she had won the lottery? That she was going to cheat on Sean? Could I hold back telling her my truth too?

I stared into her big brown eyes and my heart flipped over in my chest. No, I'd hold nothing back. The second she confessed, I'd confess too. Everything. About the lottery. About being in love with her.

"G-go on," I said, my heart beating in my throat.

She inhaled deeply and let the breath out slowly as we moved towards my car. "I don't feel as alive at any other time as I do at 2 a.m. I don't know how I'm going to deal with having to work a nine-to-five job."

All my hopes dissipated. She wasn't going to come clean. She wasn't going to tell me the truth. Jaw clenched, I moved a bit quicker and she rushed to keep up.

"What's up?" she asked as we reached my car, a note of concern in her voice.

I wanted to throw my hands up, wanted to shout, *What's up? You're going to cheat on your fiancé and here you are telling me a guilty confession about liking night-time.* It felt like a slap in the face. Hell, I wish she had hit me. That would have hurt less.

"Nothing. Just get in."

She opened the passenger door and slid in.

I plopped into the driver's seat, seething.

"Was it something I said?" she asked.

I turned the engine over and screeched out of the parking lot towards her place.

Was it something she said? No, it was something she didn't say; the fucking *truth*. Pulling in a deep breath, I struggled to fight the tide of anger rising in me. This wasn't the woman I thought I knew. She wasn't the friend I thought I had. Obviously, since she was sneaking around, lying, and cheating.

"No, I'm just in a shit mood."

Her hand came to rest on mine.

I stared at it for a second before focusing on the road. I wanted to pull away. More than that—I wanted to pull over and pull her closer. I wanted to fulfil her desires at the same time as I wanted to demand answers. It was an ugly duo that was shredding me apart inside.

"You've been off all night," she said softly, her statement sounding open-ended, an invitation to talk.

Usually I would. But not about this.

I could feel her staring at me, but I refused to look at her. She could take it personally, she could take it as a snub, or she could assume I was just trying not to kill us by watching the road...I didn't give a damn.

After a few moments of silence, her hand slipped away.

When I drove past the kebab place we usually stopped at I heard her breath hitch, but she didn't say anything.

We drove the rest of the way in silence, and when I pulled up outside her place, she turned to me like she was going to say something.

I beat her to it. "I'm going to have to pass on our usual plans this week." Like our late-night kebab ritual. Or our weekly EuroMillions lottery ticket. Hanging out in her living room till dawn.

"Oh." Her shoulders sagged. "Okay. Is everything okay?"

I could hear the hurt in her voice. As awful as it felt, I couldn't decide if it was worse than knowing I'd be the other man in her life very soon. "I'm just going to be really busy," I lied. More lies to cover the first lie. This was how mountains were made, one little cup of dirt at a time until I buried myself. "What are you going to be up to on Tuesday?" It was her day off and the day for her "date" with the four Irishmen.

She hesitated.

I prayed she was going to come clean with me.

"Um, just meeting up with a friend."

"Which friend?"

She shifted in her seat. "You don't know her, I met her at school." She'd pressed herself to the door and her hand was on the handle like escape was at the top of her mind.

"And how is Sean?" The question burst out of me.

She wouldn't meet my eyes. "Fine."

"Fine?"

"I guess."

"You *guess*?" This wasn't the woman I knew. Talking so flippantly about her boyfriend who she was planning on cheating on *with four men*, no less!

Her eyes met mine and I saw the way her lips pressed together in a thin line. "We broke up."

"*What?*"

She nodded.

"When?"

She shrugged with one shoulder. "A few weeks ago."

Oh.

Oh.

This whole time I was berating her in my head for being a cheater. But she wasn't. She was single. Of course she wasn't a fucking cheater. I knew her. I knew Aubrey.

I was such an asshole.

"Why?" An asshole who apparently could only grunt in monosyllables. *Get it together, Noah.*

She shrugged even as a sadness glossed over her eyes. "It wasn't right."

I wanted to pull her close, to hold her and stroke her hair and let her cry it out on me. I wanted to have her on my lap and when she lifted her head to look me in the eyes, I wanted to kiss her. I wanted to fucking kiss her so badly. Now that she was single…I could.

I could lean in right now and—

Fuck, I shouldn't be making moves on her right now. I schooled my features into a look of concern. This was all a friend should be feeling for her. Concern that she was okay. Not fist pumping and wanting to throw a feckin' parade because she was on the market again.

How the feck did I not see what was going on with her? How did I go several weeks—

Wait, this happened weeks ago and I was only hearing about this now?

"Why didn't you tell me?" I asked.

She let out a sigh. "I don't know. At first, I was trying to process it. It came as a shock but it kinda didn't, if that makes any sense."

It did, strangely. I never saw her and Sean lasting the length of time that they did. I almost fell off my chair when I heard they'd gotten engaged. "Are you...okay?" I studied her face, ready to pull her into my lap at the first sign of tears.

"Honestly?"

Honestly. My lies twisted in my chest. "Of course."

She chewed her lip, a clear sign she was feeling unsure. "Would it be bad if I told you I was fine?"

She was okay? She...she looked okay. More than okay. I mean, she seemed a bit preoccupied the last few weeks but nowhere near heartbroken.

She sighed, but it was filled with relief, not sadness.

"Ugh, this is why I didn't want to tell you. I was *that girl* who had agreed to marry someone I didn't really love."

"Rey..." I looked right into her eyes, "...when have I ever judged you?" *Except when I thought you were a cheater.*

She gave me a bashful look. "Never."

"So why would I start now?"

She let out a curt laugh. "Yeah, I know. Now I just feel dumb for not telling you."

I leaned in. "You know you can tell me anything, right? *Anything.*"

Like about the lottery. Here was her chance, her chance to tell me the truth I wasn't supposed to already know.

She smiled but it felt forced. "And you can tell me anything too, you know?"

This was my chance to tell her how I felt. To tell her the truth. The lottery. Everything.

I nodded, feeling my heart swell. Yes, I should go first. I'd been keeping this secret for longer. "Actually, there is something I have to tell you."

She shifted in her seat to face me. "What is it?"

I opened my mouth.

I love you.

These words jammed up in my throat and I… I couldn't force them out. I could barely breathe around them. They'd spent all these years buried so deep and now…

I've always loved you.

"Noah?" she whispered.

My name coming off her lips in that breathy tone trickled into the deepest parts of me. The silence swelled, the pressure in the car almost suffocating. A buzzing in my head started.

Dear God, man, say something.

Her tongue darted out and traced her full lower lip, drawing my gaze to it. I wanted to lean in and suck her lip into my mouth. To taste her.

"I want…" I whispered.

I wanted to give her that O. I wanted to please her all night long, close up the bar to please her all day tomorrow and the day after and after that, giving her orgasm after orgasm after orgasm until she begged me to stop. And then I'd give her one more.

"Want…what?" she asked, her sweet breath on my face.

Be with me.

I reached out and touched her chin. Tilting her head so she'd look at me. Inches. That was all that was left between us.

Her eyes widened.

If I couldn't speak the words to tell her how I felt, I'd show her. I leaned in.

Suddenly, her door popped open and she practically tumbled out of the car away from me. I felt the loss of her nearness immediately, rejection tasting bitter on my tongue.

She backed up, shutting the door between us, a strange mixture of shock and longing on her face, before bolting like a startled deer up her front steps. My heart sank as she disappeared into her building.

Fuck. I slammed my hands on the wheel. *Stupid, Noah. Too soon. Too fast. She just broke up with her fiancé, for God's sake.*

Not too early for her to be getting into bed with four strangers, a voice inside me snarked.

Maybe she just didn't want...me. This thought turned into a lump that I struggled to swallow around. Maybe I wasn't good enough for her. Maybe she really did just see me as a friend.

But that longing... I glanced up to the dark windows of her apartment. I saw that longing. I *felt* it. She wanted me to kiss her. Or at least, part of her did.

A strong urge to follow her rose in me. To knock on her door until she let me in. Demand answers. Or to kiss her until she gave in. I yanked my door handle and—

No. She needed space. Time. Rushing in was stupid. Pushing her would only send her running. I didn't want her to regret anything, and that meant letting her lead. Giving her time to be single, if that's what she wanted.

Give her the space for her feelings to grow into something more.

I could wait. I'd waited for years already. I'd wait forever for her if that's what it took.

Aubrey

I leaned against the inside of my front door, stunned, my heart beating a million times a second. Each inhale and exhale felt like I was swallowing sandpaper.

What the actual heck just happened in Noah's car?

But I knew. I knew what almost happened in Noah's car.

Noah almost kissed me.

What's worse is that I wanted him to! I wanted my best friend to kiss me. I wanted a guy—a *total player*—I swore I'd never go there with to kiss me. It'd ruin our friendship. What was wrong with me? Was I determined to lose both my fiancé *and* my best friend in a matter of weeks?

My thoughts turned back to the moment in the car. To the surge of excitement I felt at his nearness, the heat in my core as he tilted my chin and leaned in. That was brand new.

Really, Aubrey?

I lied. I'd always felt a little thrill when Noah was near but I'd never let myself *feel* it the way I had just now. I'd never admitted how real it was. It felt magnified times a thousand.

I wished I hadn't run away. I wished I'd just stayed there and enjoyed the sensations washing over me, the feeling of closeness. It was like a tide had gone out, smoothing out the distance between us over the past few weeks, leaving behind a sharp, hot tension.

I wasn't even sure what made me bolt. Maybe it was fear. Self-preservation or an instinct to preserve our friendship. If we kissed, everything would change.

Everything.

But change to what?

Noah and I were impossible. Noah didn't do relationships. He hadn't even dated anyone since I'd known him. And despite this one little lottery prize, I was a relationship kind of girl.

Oh God. The lottery prize.

My cheeks heated as I remembered that I was about to let four strangers make me come.

How could I kiss Noah with this tiny—*massive*—secret hanging between us?

No, I had to shove all these thoughts and all these feelings away and pretend it never happened. Then after my "prize" night, I'd deal with all of this…this…whatever *this* was.

And then what?

I chewed my lip. Noah could have anyone. Literally, any woman on the face of this planet, just by flashing his gorgeous grin and those trademark dimples. Why would he kiss me?

I was his best friend. He didn't see me that way. I wasn't even his type—tall, leggy, blonde and busty—basically a supermodel. Maybe he just felt sorry for me because of my break-up. He was trying to comfort me. Show me that I was still desirable or something. The way he was looking at me in the car, it certainly made me feel desirable. Like I was the most beautiful creature he'd ever seen.

He said he was going through some shit. It was probably stress over his ma. Maybe he just needed comfort from me. Yes, that was all it was. Comfort. It was stupid for me to think about the near kiss as anything more.

What would it have been like to let him kiss me? I found my fingers pressing to my tingling lips. Heat filled my core and I squeezed my thighs together like that could relieve the sudden ache there. It just made it worse. Would I have wanted him to stop at just a kiss when his eyes were promising me so much more?

My phone made a muffled beep, cutting off this dangerous line of thinking. I pulled it out of my purse still slung over my torso. It was a text from Noah.

Damn hands. They were trembling. After three tries to unlock my screen the message finally opened.

Noah: Did you make it safely?

Me: Yes, thank you.

Noah: I didn't see the light come on and I was worried.

I hadn't clicked the light on and off like I usually did, a sign that I was inside safely with the door locked. Warmth rushed through me. He cared. He'd waited even after I'd bolted. In fact, he was still sitting outside. It wasn't too late to go back down there and—

Nope. Absolutely no. Not with this *secret* hanging over my head. Present Aubrey would pretend like nothing had happened. Future Aubrey could deal with all...*this*.

I forced myself to type out a text.

Me: Thanks for caring. Good night.

Noah: Always. Good night, Rey.

Pressing my phone to my chest, I stared into the dark. *Was there something more than friendship between us? Were all the people I'd called crazy right about us?*

I shook my head to no one. *Stupid, Aubrey.* Noah was a bonafide, unapologetic player. Woman threw themselves at him all day and all night. He was relationship illiterate; he could seduce the panties off a woman, but commit to one? That he could not do.

If anything happened between Noah and me, it'd just be physical. My heart squeezed—at least, only for him. Despite his player reputation, Noah was every bit the perfect man: warm, kind, caring, funny. If I let myself, I'd fall for him. Fall hard.

It would ruin our friendship. Because I wasn't a one-night-stand kind of girl. I was a forever kind of girl. Noah was a one-night-only man.

Perhaps a part of me had always been a little in love with him. But it was like being in love with the sun. Impossible and so out of reach.

I'd always known this. So why was I getting flustered now? Why this surge of…*want* all of a sudden?

The lottery prize.

My big O.

That's why. I was getting all hot and bothered over my imminent date with four hot men. Noah was the poor sod who was getting tangled up in all these feelings. Yes, that's it.

My "date" night would alleviate the itch I was feeling. I just needed to experience a big O. It would calm the insane pull I felt towards Noah at this very moment. I could go back to only thinking of him as my best friend. A man that was perfect, but at the same time, all kinds of wrong.

The thought of my date night sent my heart knocking in my chest. I rushed to my bedroom and threw myself on my bed, squeezing my thighs together. Holy shit. I was going to be touched and pleasured by four sexy men. I'd won an encounter that very few women would ever get to experience.

For the next few days, I wouldn't stress over Sean, my visa, Noah, or anything else. I was going to live a little and enjoy life as it came.

Or...more precisely, as I came.

Aubrey

"Oh my God, amiga. Did you *hear*?" Candace yelled me as soon as I stepped into The Jar, causing every single patron to look over to her. She was standing huddled with Noah in a corner, obviously gossiping about something.

I glanced at Noah. He looked away as soon as our eyes met. Alrighty then. We were obviously ignoring the kiss that almost happened but didn't happen. I couldn't exactly avoid him without looking like a bitch to Candace. Especially with the way she was waving me over like she'd burst a blood vessel if I didn't get my ass over there right this bloody second.

I walked up to them cool, calm, confident. At least I hoped so. My feet felt like lead as I stopped in front of them. "Hey. What's up?"

"The Irish Lottery picked a winner, *lucky bitch*!"

My throat seized. *Oh, shit.* I didn't even think about it. Did they announce that it was me? Was that why Noah was avoiding my eyes? "Really?" I squeaked out.

"Nossa, amiga," Candace rattled away in a string of Portuguese that was obviously cursing. She shoved her phone screen in my face. "She is one lucky bitch."

My heart jammed into my throat as I scanned the website page on her screen. Under a heading that said *Winner Drawn, Congratulations to:* was…

A.C., Dublin

A.C.

Aubrey Campbell.

Me.

But no one could tell it was me. I mean, there were about a million A.C.s in Dublin. Well, not exactly a million but definitely a ton. More than enough to get lost in. Thank fuck.

I looked up to find Noah staring at me, a strange look on his face. Oh, shit. If anyone would figure out A.C. was me, it'd be

Noah. Don't look away. Don't look guilty. For a second it felt like he knew my secret.

"A.C.," Candace said, turning the phone to face her. "I need to hunt this bitch down and high five her, the lucky *puta*." An evil grin spread over her features. "Then kill her and take her place."

Noah let out a laugh as he turned to Candace.

I sagged with relief now that I was out of his keen focus.

"You won't find her," he said.

"I will."

"A.C. probably isn't even her real initials."

"What?"

"I mean, the internet makes it so easy for her to *lie*."

Even though Noah wasn't looking at me, I felt his words like they were arrows aimed at my chest.

Candace let out a sniff. "Regardless whether her initials are real or not, someone will find out who she is."

"No," I said, my voice going all hollow, blood draining from my limbs.

"How would they possibly find out? The whole lottery is anonymous." Noah's calm logic was like a balm over me.

"Please…" Candace said, waving her phone about. "Everyone is trying to find out who the Irish Lottery foursome are. There are forums of armchair detectives who have blown up the image, trying to squirrel out who these guys are based on birthmarks or mole placements. Others are trying to find clues in the reflection of the boys' eyes."

Holy shit. There were some clever people around. I wouldn't have even thought of doing that. And persistent. Terror crept across me. I fought like hell to stop it from showing. They couldn't know. No one could know.

"Has anyone come up with anything useful?" Noah asked, voicing the question thundering through my brain.

Candace's shoulders sagged. "Well, no. But that doesn't mean they won't."

"I doubt it. If they haven't figured it out by now, they won't." Noah chuckled and patted Candace's shoulder before he walked off.

A miffed-looking Candace turned to me. "I don't care what Noah says. Once they find the guys, it's only a matter of time before they find out who the winner is."

Aubrey

I woke up with a strange sensation between my thighs and a heartbeat that seemed elevated. My body felt sensitized, like I'd suddenly tuned in to the right frequency and I could feel *everything*. The air on my skin, the sheets under my body.

Today was O day.

O day. I felt like I should throw a parade. Make it a national holiday. O's for everyone!

With a little happy dance, I turned on the shower. I'd be lying if I said I wasn't enjoying having the place to myself. With my roomie staying at her boyfriend's house for the night, I knew there wouldn't be any interruptions. Under slick needles of hot water, I scrubbed every inch of my body with my favorite body wash, something delicately vanilla scented. My heart pounded in my chest so hard I could feel every thud at the base of my throat. I swallowed back the excitement that kept creeping up my windpipe. I needed to shave my legs, wash my hair, pluck my eyebrows.

I needed to be calm.

My mind sent up an image of the four masked men, thoughts lingering on the blue-eyed one. Heat blossomed in my chest. I exhaled on a soft moan as my whole body reacted. Goosebumps prickled down my arms, my nipples tightened, aching for contact.

Quick on the heels of this sensual feeling was a wave of guilt. Noah's face surfaced in my mind. After the near kiss, I'd managed to spend a hot minute fantasizing that he actually wanted me. Not that he was just looking for comfort like I'd decided. I'd imagined him telling me in that throaty voice that he wanted to make me come, I'd imagined looking into his piercing eyes and falling off the edge of that glorious cliff.

It was ridiculous. No, it was downright stupid. Noah and I were just friends. *Best friends.*

I deserved this fantasy. My body, my life. I wasn't hurting anyone. I was a consenting adult. And it's not like Noah has ever, *ever* expressed wanting anything more than friendship from me.

With an annoyed noise in my throat, I began to shave my legs. It was my day to enjoy myself. Torturing myself over my best friend didn't factor into that. Banishing the last bit of guilt that I felt, I continued to get ready.

When I was clean, dry and silky smooth, I put on the lingerie I'd bought just for tonight, the silky material causing goosebumps as it travelled up my legs and over my body. I'd been torn between something naughty and sexy or something more on the innocent side. I'd gone with the one that felt true to me.

I applied minimal makeup, a touch of liner to the corners of my eyes to give me a slightly sultry look, then lengthened my lashes with dark mascara.

When I was done, I stared at myself in the mirror. I could barely recognize myself.

The two-piece lingerie was pure white, the off-the-shoulder top trimmed in lace covered most of my breasts but gave a clear view of the underside of them. It flowed to my hips and everything below the lace trim was see-through white to the hem. The white lace panties cut high on my hips, making my legs look longer.

My eyes looked hooded and dark, my cheeks flushed, hair falling down over my shoulders. I looked like a sensual, sexual, confident woman. I felt beautiful and sexy.

I was so ready.

Noah

My brothers were chatting around me, but I couldn't focus on their words. We were in the car right now on the way to Aubrey's place.

I checked my phone again. The minutes were ticking by. The chance for her to come clean and tell me the truth was vanishing with every second we spent in the car.

"Jaysus, you're not going to puke, are you?" Michael asked me from the back seat where he sat with Eoin.

"If he bows out sick, I'll take his place," Eoin said.

A hot flare shot through my gut. I wanted to climb back there and punch Eoin's face in. Instead, I flexed my fist and glared out the window.

High-octane energy flowed through the car. I could feel how on edge everyone was.

Behind the wheel, Darren was driving fast, his attention locked on the road. His jaw was tight and rippling like he was chewing on thoughts he didn't want to share.

In the back seat, the fight between Michael and Eoin stepped up a notch. Michael grunted and it was assumed Eoin had gotten him with a sneaky elbow. They'd been sparring this morning at the gym, trying to beat the shit out of one another with gloves and protection on.

I wasn't sure what was fueling the feud between them, but I had a feeling there was something going on there. Something I wasn't aware of.

I hoped they'd gotten all that roughness out of their systems before we got to Aubrey. Brothers or not, if they hurt her, I'd kill them myself.

I, on the other hand, had lagged in my workout this morning. I felt…numb. Disconnected.

"Fucking knock it off back there," Darren barked sharply.

The noise and motion in the back seat ceased. For all of two seconds. I heard Michael exhale hard and knew Eoin must have landed a good blow to his ribs. Then they were back at it.

"I'll pull this shit over and kick both your asses," Darren growled.

"You wouldn't," Eoin said. "Then we'd be late."

"He wouldn't risk that," Michael said, sounding every bit as childish as Eoin in that moment.

"The fuck I wouldn't," Darren said. "Don't test me, boy."

Once more there was silence from the back seat.

"The fuck? He thinks he our da?" Eoin grumbled.

Everyone ignored him.

I stared out the window, thinking about Aubrey, my heart beating faster the closer we got to her place.

I was going to see her naked.

I was going to touch her.

Watch her come.

I swallowed hard. I'd secretly dreamed of this for years. Aubrey was sexy as hell, in that quiet way of hers. Not a loud, obviously sexy like Candace. Aubrey didn't realize how gorgeous she was. I'd kept my feelings in check all these years, but they'd been there all along, coloring my friendship with her with secret desire.

The fact that my dream was about to become a reality was only overshadowed by the fact that she wouldn't know it was me behind that mask. A quiet voice inside me said that I was betraying her in a way.

I shoved that thought aside. Aubrey might never look at me that way unless I showed her how good we could be together. I mean, she practically ran from me when I tried to kiss her the other night. I was just her best friend, but behind the mask, I could be her lover. Her man. The one she *wanted*.

After all this time of dreaming about her and fantasizing about her, I was going to taste her lips. Taste her. Touch her. Hell, it was everything I ever wanted. Mostly everything I ever wanted, anyway.

A tight grin tugged at the corners of my lips. She had no idea what we had in store for her. She was going to have her O, alright. And I couldn't fucking wait to give her one. Ten. Thirty. As many as I could coax, persuade, and pull from her body. I wasn't going to stop making her come until she begged for mercy. Even then, I might have to give her one more.

Part of me hated that my brothers would also be there. But I trusted them. Even Eoin. He might have teased me about going after her, but I knew in my heart he never would. We had a plan.

Pleasing Aubrey was first and foremost in my mind. This was what she wanted. What she'd asked for.

I'd do damn near anything to make her happy.

Slipping on our green masks, we headed for her front door.

Michael pushed me forward. I was the leader in this and I needed to get it under control.

I took in a deep breath. And knocked. Silence swelled out around me. Would she answer? Did she change her mind?

I saw the peephole darken. I could swear I heard a sharp intake of breath. She was there. Right there on the other side of this wood panel. The second she opened the door, it'd change everything.

Everything.

No going back. No hiding my feelings from her anymore. Fuck. My stomach jumbled up into untangleable knots. Was I really doing this?

Too late. I heard the *snick* of the door unlocking. I could hardly breathe as the door swung open.

Aubrey stood there, partly hidden behind the door she was clinging onto for support. The whole world ceased to exist as I drank in the sight of her. Her white lingerie was as pure as driven snow. The swell of her breasts, playing peek-a-boo under the lace, had me harder than I'd ever been in my damn life.

My cock pulsed painfully. She looked better than I could have ever imagined. Sexier than any woman I'd ever seen naked. Her soft hair tumbled free around her face and shoulders invitingly. The nervous way she chewed her lip had me wanting to groan. Even her bare feet and pink painted toenails were a turn-on.

She was fucking perfect.

Her eyes, wide with terror and excitement, locked onto mine. Her name was on my tongue, ready to be exhaled.

But I kept it to myself. I could not give myself away. Not yet.

Aubrey

All four of the masked men were eyeing me with heated appreciation. But Blue Eyes was staring at me more intensely than the others, awe shining out from his face. I couldn't take my eyes off him.

He stepped closer as one of the others nudge-pushed him forward.

I stumbled back, my lungs tightening as they all crowded into my apartment. Every drop of saliva in my mouth dried up.

Someone locked the door behind them with a click.

Holy shit. Was this really happening?

I could hardly breathe, feeling like they were stealing all the air. They were bigger in real life than the image had led me to believe. I supposed that several big, tall guys didn't seem as imposing when they were only around other big, tall guys. But seeing them now, towering over me, fear crept in. Louder than fear was excitement pounding through my body with every drum of my heartbeat.

"Hi. Hey," I heard myself mumbling. "Hi, um…" I'd said hi already.

What do I do now? Did I offer them a drink?

Dear God, Aubrey. They're here to pleasure you, not for afternoon tea.

Oh, shit. They were here for *me*.

Warmth pooled low in my core. I felt like prey standing before a pack of wolves ready to tear me apart. Every nerve ending in my body was popping off, a rapid fire of heat and prickling, tingling excitement that had me on edge and my senses on high alert. It was exhilarating. Terrifying. I wanted to run but I was frozen to the spot.

Blue Eyes seemed to sense my apprehension. He smiled, warm and comforting. Like he was telling me, *we got this. We got you.*

I felt calm for all of one second.

Before the four of them advanced on me.

THE IRISH LOTTERY

Aubrey

They surrounded me.

Blue Eyes was front and center, taking up my vision. I couldn't see the others but I could feel them all around me, feel their body heat pressing in close. I could smell the mix of male scents that invaded every breath and overwhelmed me.

Hands gripped my hips from behind, running up my sides towards my breasts. More hands on my thighs, my hips, my stomach.

A squeak of surprise escaped me as hands found the intimate flesh between my thighs but not quite touching me *there*. Fingers trailed the swell of my breasts. A hand trailed up my breastbone to my throat.

My pulse was pounding in my ears, I couldn't hear anything but my heartbeat. I couldn't feel anything but the overload of touch. My body screamed and begged for more even as my knees threatened to give out and leave me in a puddle at their feet.

Blue Eyes hadn't put his hands on me yet. He was just watching me, his eyes flaring with hunger at every noise that escaped me. Maybe it was because he was holding back, but I craved his touch more than anyone else's.

"Do something," I whispered to him. "Please."

His nostrils flared. His fingers came up to grip my chin and tilt up my face. Looking back, I should have known right then, should have recognized this familiar touch. He leaned in, pausing an inch away from my lips and exhaling before he claimed my mouth.

I had no thought as he kissed me. No name. I was lost in the way his lips moved against mine, the sweep of his tongue and the taste of mint.

He sucked the last little bit of worry and fear from me and I relaxed in his arms, in all their hands.

As if this was the cue, I felt the hands on me go from gentle to sure. Over my breasts, pinching at my pebbled nipples, curving over my backside. Mouths joined the hands, teeth tagging, tongues tasting, leaving slightly damp spots that cooled quickly and heightened the sensations running wild through me.

Blue Eyes pulled his mouth off me and I let out a whimper.

My top was tugged up and off me, my heavy breasts falling exposed. My panties were slipped down my thighs by two hands of different men in unison like it had been planned, further heightening my excitement.

Instinctively, I made a move to cross my arms in front of me, to hide my sudden nakedness. But hands from behind me gripped my arms just above my elbows, locking my arms slightly behind me, forcing me to push my chest out to Blue Eyes as though I was being presented to him.

He let out a groan as his gaze brushed across my body, causing my nipples to harden to near painful.

I felt so vulnerable.

Exposed.

Yet totally and utterly safe.

I heard the clink of belts and rustle of clothing being removed around me. But I couldn't take my eyes off Blue, who was stripping off his shirt with one hand.

I sucked in a breath. He was more beautiful than I remembered from the website image. Broad, rounded shoulders…thick, muscled torso…smooth, lightly tanned skin that begged to be touched.

Blue traced light fingers from my chin down the swells of my body, wildfire igniting along his gasoline touch. Before he stepped in close, close enough that I could feel how hard he was and how hot his skin was, he kissed me again.

With greedy hands I touched the wide plains of his chest, luxuriating in the rough patch of golden hair in the center, before running them down the ridges of his six-pack. Just…wow.

Everywhere around me I could feel the heat of skin, the firmness of toned muscle. I knew that every single one of these men was as gorgeous as Blue. Hands and mouths continued to explore my body until I was shaking. I could feel their restraint and wished they'd lose control and just put me out of my misery.

I wanted them to touch me *there*.

But they didn't.

They came close.

Achingly.

Teasingly.

Close.

Again and again.

Until I could feel my wetness slick across the insides of my thighs. Until I was moaning, gasping, pleading into the mouth of the one with blue eyes.

He growled and I felt him push away the hands that were holding back my arms. His arms replaced them as my prison, wrapping around me like a vice and lifting me up against him. Instinctively I wrapped my legs around him. We let out twin groans as my naked wetness pressed against his clothed hard-on.

He carried me through my apartment to my bedroom, the others right behind. Looking back, I should have wondered how he already knew where to go. But I was too lost in the depths of his ocean blues as he carried me to my bed like I weighed nothing. He kneeled on the mattress and placed me on the neatly made spread.

Oh, God.

This was really happening.

I thought he might stay there between my legs, but he didn't. He moved aside and laced his fingers with mine, pressing my hand into the bed as he kissed my neck. On my other side, another one grabbed my wrist and held me captive before diving towards a breast. More hands held open my thighs. One of them growled with approval as I lay exposed to him, writhing helplessly under the palms and mouths of his friends.

I expected to feel fear at being pinned and at their mercy. Instead, I felt safe and warm and wanted.

So wanted. More wanted than I'd ever felt before.

One of them kneeled between my legs as he began to explore me, using his fingertips to stroke me from entrance to clit. Every pass sent more liquid heat through me, and I quickly found myself moving with him, moving my hips in time to him.

Someone's lips closed around my nipple and I cried out, my back arching as the one between my legs sped up his torturously slow stroking. Electricity bolted through my belly sending shockwaves of warmth radiating through me that collided with the pleasure I felt from the skilled fingers working between my thighs.

Lost in the moment, in the ecstasy, I squeezed my eyes closed and arched my back, silently begging them all for more, more, more.

I'd never been more turned on in my life. I'd never experienced anything like this. Didn't realize it could feel this good. I heard myself begging them pitifully not to stop around moans of pure pleasure.

Was this what I'd been missing? Was this what sex was supposed to be?

Between my legs, the stroking had sped up and I could feel a thumb on my clit working circles with my own moisture. I should be embarrassed at how wet I was. But in that moment, nothing mattered except for the edge which I was barreling towards.

I started bucking, wanting to hurry it up. Hands pinned my hips down, easily holding me immobile.

These four strangers could do whatever they wanted with me.

The pinch of fear spiced my pleasure in a way I never thought I'd like and felt a bit ashamed to admit.

The fingers circling between my legs sped up. Teeth nibbled on my earlobe and hands continued to roam every inch of me with more pressure than before. But I...couldn't.

"Just let go," Blue whispered in my ear, his voice rough and low.

I turned my head to lock eyes with him. That was all I needed. I cried out as everything tightened up, my whole body bearing down so tightly I felt near pain. Pleasure imploded deep in my core.

I lay there, trembling as aftershocks attacked me. There was a shift and I felt very wet lips on my hip and thigh and knew the one that had brought me to orgasm had traded places with someone else.

Slowly, the mouth moved up my thigh. I thought I might not be able to take any more, but the soft kisses only seemed to bring my need back to life.

It wasn't possible. I couldn't want *more* again so soon, could I? I heard a moan coming from me as his mouth neared my pussy, hands continuing to stroke every inch of the rest of me. Apparently, I could.

Finally, the second man, stretched out on his belly between my legs, licked his tongue across my slit, causing me to cry out. He licked me again and again.

His fingers pressed aside the flesh on either side of my clit, his green eyes watching me from between my legs, a smirk on his lips before he formed a seal around my throbbing button. White hot pleasure seared through me. He teased the little bundle of nerves between his lips, with his teeth and the tip of his tongue.

I was moaning, struggling to buck. I barely recognized myself, acting like a hungry little slut, so desperate for more.

I didn't care. I *was* desperate. I needed this. And it felt better than I'd ever imagined.

Bolts of electricity shot through my core from the magical spot his tongue was working. My body was gathering, tightening, and with every second ticking by I knew I was closer and closer.

"Please don't stop," I begged as my belly tightened up.

"Close again already?" someone growled.

"Oh, God." It's all I could manage to get out.

The whole world exploded in white and I let out a long, low howl as pleasure ripped through my core. I could feel my body squeezing so tightly it ached as ripple after ripple of pleasure washed over me.

The lips and tongue on me eased up a lot as if he knew how oversensitive the spot was. "So sweet," he mumbled as he ran his tongue up me, tasting me one last time.

I wanted to lift my head, to look at him, to look at them all, but all I could do was stare at the ceiling as my body melted into a puddle in the middle of my bed.

I felt certain every inch of me had been touched, every bit of exposed flesh had been kissed and licked, and I couldn't recall a time I'd felt as pampered, as sexy, as desired. All these men wanted me, I could feel it in their touches, hear it in their deep moans and growls. I'd never been so out of control of my body, never been so totally in someone else's control. It was freeing and sexy and *incredible.*

Suddenly, the whole world shifted as the third man grabbed me and did a quick movement almost like a wrestler. Suddenly, I was on top of him. A hand fisted in my hair and gently pulled back while others were lifting my shoulders and sitting me upright. The man under me was naked and I could feel a barrier between us. They'd thought to use protection.

His green eyes locked on me as he adjusted himself. I'd expected him to enter me, but he didn't. He merely settled himself between my folds and grabbed my hips. Suddenly, I was moving, rubbing on him in a way that had me tossing my head back and moaning. It was incredible, just the right amount of pleasure and excitement.

Hands teased my breasts, fingertips dug into my skin, and I could feel them being overly intimate without invading me once more. Excitement thundered through me and I could feel my heart beating so hard I wondered if it was going to break my breastbone.

I tried to tilt my hips as my body demanded more, tried to take him inside me, but he shifted and prevented me from getting the angle I needed. With a whimper of disappointment that quickly shifted to excitement as hands began to tease and pinch and roll my nipples once more, I found myself bucking and moving harder, faster, headlong towards yet another orgasm. I could feel his erection getting harder and harder as I slid over it. The way his fingertips dug into my hips left me worried about bruises tomorrow. I realized I didn't give a damn. Let them bruise me. Let them mark me. No one else would see but me, and I sure as hell wouldn't mind the reminder.

A hand found my throat, holding but not squeezing, and another set of fingers grabbed a palmful of my backside and squeezed.

All the sensations met in my center and my vision went white. The whole world ceased as pleasure rolled through me. My hips bucked erratically and I felt them holding me up, keeping me moving, supporting me with strong arms and powerful hands as the third orgasm tore through my being.

I sagged but didn't fall. I could hear their whispers and growls even though my broken brain couldn't make heads or tails of what they were saying.

Suddenly, I was scooped up and laid back on the bed.

I lifted my head as the door closed behind three of the men. I was alone with the blue-eyed one. The only one yet to bring me to orgasm. Dazed and trembling, I could only whimper as I stared up at him, wondering what he had in store for me and praying I could withstand it.

Aubrey

His eyes were fiercely blue like the center of twin flames, hot with desire.

"Who are you?" I whispered, wanting to know at the same time *not*.

I knew that the NDA was supposed to protect them from me saying anything, but I hadn't expected them to still wear their masks. Part of me liked it. Liked the anonymity. Like they could brush past me along one of Dublin's cobbled lanes tomorrow and I wouldn't know it.

He didn't respond and I wondered what he had in store for me. I shivered. He was just studying me like I was the most beautiful creature he'd ever seen. How could this stranger feel so comfortable and...familiar?

Three orgasms. I'd had three. Three mind-blowing orgasms. Yet some part of me whispered that the best was yet to come.

I hadn't expected it to be like this. I hadn't really had any idea what would happen, but I expected a lot more sex. They'd all been very careful not to fuck me and that was the one thing I was wanting more than anything else in that moment.

Blue gently pressed me back down onto the bed. I followed his silent instructions. My whole body was still humming with pleasure and excitement, and he parted my knees and slid between them, pressing his moist lips to the inside of my thigh, moving up bit by bit. It didn't feel like he was trying to please me; it felt like he was *worshiping* me.

Squeezing my eyes closed, I fisted my hands into the bedspread, silently praying he'd keep going. His lips stopped high up on my inner thigh, just shy of the part of me that was tingling and swollen. I let out a pleading moan.

His lips pressed to my other thigh and worked down towards my knee.

"Teasing bastard," I murmured.

He chuckled against my skin, sending tremors through my

body, my heart jackhammering in my chest.

How was I not cooling off now that there was only one man? For some reason being alone with him was even more overwhelming than having all four of them on me at once. Instead of scattered sensations, all my senses were intensified as they focused on him. I could feel the outline of his lips pressing against my skin, the brush of his breath. Each sensation leaving my breath shuddering.

His lips halted at the inside of my knee before he nibbled and licked his way back towards the center of me. I lifted my hips in anticipation. This time he didn't disappoint. His lips pressed to my sensitive flesh, a gasp escaping me.

I wanted to start moving, to grind myself on his face and release the building tension in me. But his hands snaked behind my thighs and pressed flat to my hips, pinning me down in a way that sent a thrill through me.

His tongue parted me with one long, sensual lick. I shivered, a moan ripping from my throat. He did it again, just as slowly, just as torturously, his tongue lapping the length of my entrance, looping around my swollen, hypersensitive clit before going down.

Again.

Again.

And…again.

With every pass a wave of warmth and pleasure rolled through my belly, crashing over every nerve ending.

This was different. The other men had been racing to get me over the edge. But Blue didn't seem as worried about the ending as the journey. I was a goddess and he was *worshiping* me. He licked me like he loved the taste of me, like he couldn't get enough. The way he watched me from between my legs, collecting all of my gasps and moans like they were precious gems.

Tears stung in my eyes. It had never been like this with Sean. Or the two guys before him. Sean never went out of his way to give me pleasure. Sex felt rushed, to be done with quickly like it was wrong and he didn't want to get caught. He'd never lay me on top of the sheets, reverently open my legs to the heavens and make love to my flesh with his mouth.

That's what this felt like.

I'd never felt so wanted. So beautiful. So loved.

It took a stranger with the most gorgeous blue eyes to show me that this was possible. That this was what I'd been missing. What I deserved.

I wanted to thank Blue, to pour out my heart to him, but some words are too valuable. Too precious. These admissions were delicate butterflies made from parts of my soul, not meant for strangers. That's what Blue was to me—a stranger, I had to keep reminding myself. One I'd probably never see again.

I reached up towards his head instead.

He stiffened.

"I just want to touch you," I whispered. "I won't take the mask off. I promise."

He relaxed into my fingers threading through his hair. So soft between my fingers. With care, I pushed aside threads of hair stuck to his forehead, ran my fingers along his scalp like I was writing out my secrets just for him. All the while, his stare burned into me.

I wanted desperately to push off his mask, to know the man who was loving my body like I'd never been loved before. But I didn't. I'd promised him. I couldn't betray him like that. We were strangers but...somehow, we felt *right*. Like our bodies knew each other from before somehow.

He made a low noise in his throat. The vibration hit my clit like a bolt of pure lightning. An orgasm crashed through me before I even knew it was coming. I let out a stunned cry as everything faded out and the only sense I had was *pleasure*.

I came to, finding him kneeling between my legs, his eyes still on me, his chin glossy with my wetness. His fingers played along my entrance before sliding into me in a long, gentle stroke.

His fingers pressed a bit harder into me, touching something magical inside.

With every push of his fingers everything started gearing up again. Somehow, he took me from finished to climbing again right away. It was so effortless I couldn't figure out how he did it. How did he know my body better than I knew it myself? It just didn't seem possible.

His thumb parted my flesh easily and began to work slow, maddening circles around my button. I could hear myself, hear my pitiful little whining moans and gasps as the pleasure began to intensify. *Again.*

Dear God. Were the four orgasms I'd had not enough?

My insides clamped down and I cried out in pleasure. I felt his hand clamp down on my mouth as a near scream ripped out of me. "Shhh," he growled in a tone more animal than man.

His hand left my mouth as the orgasm faded. I let out a long sigh. If he stopped now, I could be satisfied.

The whole bed shifted as he stood at the side of the bed. He finally pushed off his jeans. My gaze dropped to his naked body. He was glorious. Like a living statue of David. He tore a small packet I hadn't noticed in his hand before rolling it over his length.

Oh, shit. He was...big.

His lips lifted in a smirk before he climbed naked over me and lowered his naked body onto mine. Our twin groans filled my ears.

I lied. I would not be satisfied until he was inside me. I needed to feel him press into me, wanted to feel my body stretch around him. I wanted to feel *him* come.

He had other plans, though. He slid his cock between us in that maddening way that shoved me headlong towards yet another orgasm. My heartrate doubled. My eyes rolled back as my hips began to move against his to match his rhythm. A maddening rhythm that promised so much more.

This wasn't enough. I wanted *him*.

My eyes snapped open and locked onto his eyes blazing into mine. Maybe he didn't want to sleep with me?

"Don't you want...*me*?" I asked.

He nodded, a tight, controlled motion that made something flutter in my belly. His jaw tight. I realized then how much control he was exerting. He did want me. He wanted me badly. He was holding himself back from entering me as he slid himself between us.

I realized what he was doing. He was giving me every form of the first three orgasms I'd had, but with his own particular style. Like he was painting over them, wiping over my memory of them with him—*only him*.

"Please, fuck me," I begged.

But he refused. As he rocked against me, his lips pressed to my throat, followed by the slight sting of his teeth scraping the delicate flesh there. I was on the edge, teetering between sanity and total destruction.

Suddenly, the world imploded and I cried out, arching my back, my nails digging into his shoulders as I clung onto him like he was the only thing tethering me to this earth. "Oh, my God," I breathed. My eyelids fluttered open to find two blue irises in the center of my world.

"Are you okay?" he growled.

I nodded. I'd never been more okay in my life.

I felt him shift, felt the head of him press against me. He paused. I wrapped my legs around him, telling him it was okay, telling him I wanted him. More than anything.

He leaned down to kiss me. This time his kiss was soft, gentle, loving as he eased into me inch by inch, stretching me around him. We both exhaled as he slid in to the hilt.

I could feel his heartbeat against mine, smell the thick, spicy scent of him. I felt safe, loved, and secure.

My beautiful Blue. Perfect stranger. I don't know your name and I probably will never see you again, but being with you has changed me.

Thank you.

I will never forget you.

Noah

All logic and reason had vacated my brain. Seeing Aubrey come over and over and over again was a slow descent into beautiful madness. Sliding into her warm body shattered that last wall I'd had up between us.

I was hers.

And she was mine.

Her body was so responsive, like it was made for me. How had that douche never given her an orgasm? It was so easy, so quick I almost felt like I'd cheated her. I didn't want to stop. Not now, not ever.

I began to move, sliding my length in and out of her. Fuck, she felt like heaven. She moaned into my mouth and I chased each one trying to catch them like falling raindrops. Her hands fisting into the sheets, my arms caging her face.

She was glorious surrender.

She was war and peace.

She was home. My home.

I loved her more than I could even admit to myself, let alone to her.

Though, if I'm honest, I had admitted as much to her. She just didn't know it. Every touch, every stroke, kiss, lick, every orgasm I gave her was an admission.

I might have been wearing a mask, but in my heart, I was naked.

"Oh, God," she said in that sweet voice of hers.

She was going to come again and I couldn't wait. I wanted a lifetime of making her come. I wanted forever revering her. I wanted to adore every inch of her body like this for the rest of our damn lives.

I pulled her knees up higher, tilted my hips so I would hit that spot inside of her. And I fucked her, hard. Desperately.

Like this orgasm would make her mine.

Mine.

I slammed into her, loving the way she gasped and cussed. Sexy and cute all rolled into one. And pressure was building, my mind was unravelling and she was tightening up and—

She let out a scream as her body convulsed around me. I couldn't hold back anymore. I came, hard.

"Rey!" burst from my lips.

I felt her whole body stiffen.

Just like that, on the heels of the most intense pleasure I'd ever experienced, I knew that everything had just fallen apart.

She recognized my voice.

Aubrey

I knew that voice.

It wasn't possible. My lungs squeezed so hard I couldn't breathe. I froze for a second, but only for a second.

He cursed and pushed himself up to kneeling, holding his hands out in surrender. "I can explain."

Noah's voice.

My best friend's voice.

My heart began to pound so hard in my chest it throbbed. I backed up on the bed and yanked the blankets up to cover myself.

Mortified. I was absolutely *mortified*.

I stared into his familiar blue eyes. Noah's eyes. The line of his jaw, his chin, the broad shoulders. All the little things I should have recognized stood out now, mocking me.

How had I not recognized him? How had I not known from the very first second that Noah was Blue?

Because I never thought my best friend would keep something so fucking huge from me.

He was behind the infamous Irish Lottery. And he never told me.

He knew I'd won. And he never told me.

He just fucked me and…

How could he do this to me?

Why would he do this to me?

Suddenly, things started falling into place. His standoffish behavior in the car, him asking about Sean, asking me what I was doing tonight. He'd been testing me.

"Why?" I forced out.

"To raise enough money…Ma…" he trailed off.

Oh, fuck.

Oh, my God. My cheeks flared as a realization hit me square in the chest. "The other three were…" I trailed off. I could see very well in the shame on Noah's face that I was right.

The three other guys. They weren't friends of Noah's; they were his *brothers*.

Eoin.

Michael.

Darren.

Suddenly, I saw them in my mind hidden behind their masks. Their frames, the way they moved. I'd spent enough time with them that I knew them. It was so obvious now.

All three of them had seen me naked. Touched me. One of them knew the taste of my pussy, the second had his fingers inside me, the third knew the feeling of my pussy sliding along his cock. They'd all made me come.

What the actual fuck? A voice inside me screamed.

I swallowed back bile. Had I even won legitimately?

I couldn't get past the unbelievable coincidence that out of thousands of people who entered this contest, *I'd* been chosen at random.

I was chosen. On purpose.

Was it all set up so they could get me into bed? *All four of them?* Was this some kind of sick brotherly pact?

Tears stung my eyes and I sucked in a deep, pained breath as it all hit me. I'd just had the best sex of my life. With Noah! With my best friend.

"You bastard," I hissed.

Noah flinched as if I'd slapped him. "Rey—"

"No fucking way this is a coincidence."

"It was. I swear."

Lies. He was lying to me now just like he was lying to me then. I shook my head, trying to shake this whole situation out of my vision. Trying to wake myself up from this bad dream.

Some part of me begged for this to all be a joke. A mistake. If it was a joke, it was the sickest, most twisted, fucked up joke anyone had ever pulled in the history of mankind.

Noah and his brothers read my entry. They read my fantasy. *I just want someone to make me come.* My insides burned. How they must have laughed.

"Rey—"

"Did you and you brothers laugh over my entry? Laugh over how pathetic I was?"

"No! We would never. Your entry broke my heart that—"

"You fucked me because you felt sorry for me?"

"What? No!"

"Poor Aubrey. Can't find her O. Can't keep a man who gives enough of a shit to give her one."

"That's not what happened."

They fucking saw me naked. Saw me come. Made me come, over and over again.

"Are they outside now, high fiving each other?"

"No!" He looked horrified.

"And after tonight? Were you four going to walk away from me and keep me in the dark?" *His brothers* had brought me to orgasm and Noah had let them. They had seen me naked, heard the noises I made when I fell apart. How could I ever face anyone in that family ever again? "I'd have to see you again—you *all* again—at your fucking ma's house for Sunday lunch and sit at a table where every single man there had made me come?" I was shrieking now.

"No! I was going to tell you..." He trailed off, guilt flashing across his features.

How could I ever trust him again? How could I ever even look at him again without feeling betrayed?

"When? Before or after you made me come for the seventh fucking time?"

"Aubrey, please," he begged. He snatched off his mask and moved towards me.

The sight of his face—Noah's face, my best friend's face— made me wail. Before now I could almost pretend it was someone else behind the mask. This made it all too real.

He reached out for me.

"Don't touch me," I said. I planted a hand on his warm, bare shoulder and shoved him. The same shoulder I'd been gripping as I came not all that long ago. The shoulder I'd cried on. That I used to lean on.

Was it all a lie? Was he ever really my friend? Or had he spent this whole time waiting for the right moment to make me another notch in his bedpost?

That couldn't be true. I knew Noah. He was a good man, a—

The Noah I knew wouldn't have fucked me while pretending to be a stranger.

"Rey—"

I shook my head.

I didn't want to hear it. None of it. I didn't want to hear his excuses. I didn't need him to explain it to me. I didn't want to hear his justifications or his reasons.

It was too little too late. Wrapped in my blanket, pain flowered in my chest and I felt my chin begin to quiver. It all ached so much I couldn't breathe, my heart shattering into a billion shards.

I'd been betrayed by the best friend I had in this world.

I should have seen it. I should have known the second I saw those incredible blue eyes.

"*Get out.*"

There was a long pause. Where Noah looked like he wanted to say something.

I didn't want to talk anymore. There was nothing to say. Nothing that would make much difference. He couldn't very well un-fuck me, now could he? He couldn't un-ruin our friendship. He couldn't un-break my trust in him. He couldn't un-lie to me or un-trick me.

I couldn't stand to look at him anymore so I buried my face in the blankets.

I felt the bed shift as he got up. Heard him moving around the room, the rustle of clothes as he got dressed.

I would not cry.

I wouldn't.

I heard the bedroom door click shut behind him. The echo of the front door.

I was left alone in my bedroom that still smelled of sex and of Noah.

Over his scent, the smell of his betrayal lingered.

Noah

Stunned, I stepped out of Aubrey's building onto the sidewalk. The door slammed closed behind me. The wind hit me hard, plastering my clothing to me, but I didn't feel the chill I knew should come with it. I didn't feel anything except numb. Which was a fucking shame considering all the pleasure I'd just experienced watching her writhe in ecstasy. Seeing her whole face shift as she neared the edge, the excitement and joy as she plunged over the edge...

I'd never seen a woman look half as sexy as she did naked,

vulnerable and raw for me. I loved her little breathy gasps, her cries, her moans. I loved every fucking bit of it *because I fucking loved her.*

Now, all the pleasure I'd felt, all the incredible sensations of touching her, pleasing her, watching her come over and over again…it was all gone. Decimated.

I stared out into the quiet street without really seeing any of it. It didn't seem possible that only a few hours earlier we were all piling out from the car in that spot on the curb and heading up the stairs to Aubrey's place.

The car was gone now, but I expected that. The plan, after all, had been for my brothers to leave me with Aubrey and just go. No doubt they'd gone to a bar to celebrate a job well done and the victory that we could actually pay for Ma's surgery. I could imagine them all clapping each other on the back, downing pints and shouting their victory yells. The thought of joining them wasn't appealing. I didn't feel like celebrating. I sure as hell didn't want to explain why I wasn't spending the night with Aubrey as we'd planned. That plan had gone to hell.

Fuck, I felt like such an asshole. Even now, the images stuck circling my brain were all of her. The glitter of tears clinging to her lashes. That hunched set to her shoulders like I'd fucking *broken* her. The way she'd recoiled from my touch, hiding underneath blankets like she couldn't even bear to let me see her naked. The look of agony in her eyes as she refused to even look at me.

Every single image ate away at me.

I wanted to turn back round, walk right back up those damn

steps to her place. I wanted to open her door, walk through her apartment and gather her up into my arms. I wanted to hold her until she stopped hitting me and fighting me, until she just melted into me and cried out all her fury and frustrations so we could talk this shite out. I wanted to fix it. I wanted to make it right.

I wanted to tell her I was sorry. I was sorry for hurting her. I was wrong that I thought what I had been doing was for the best.

But I wasn't sorry for the passion we'd shared. I wasn't sorry for bringing her pleasure. I wasn't sorry for making love to her, because that's what I had done.

She needed to know it was the best damned night of my life.

I spun on my heels and stared at her front door, closed and silent like it was mocking me. I lifted my hand to press her buzzer and froze—

The venom in her voice as she told me to *get out* burned at the back of my throat. She'd never spoken that way to me before. But then again, I'd never tricked her into sleeping with me before. I winced. That wasn't what it was. But that's what it must have looked like to her. My stomach churned and I thought I might be sick right there on her doorstep.

Maybe she was angry now but…she'd forgive me, right? I mean, she was my best friend.

I just needed a sign. A sign that we'd get through this. We'd be okay, right?

I tilted my head back to look up to the windows of her

apartment. I don't know what I was expecting. That she'd be standing at the window looking down at me, wishing that I would come back. That her light would be on, a sign that there was still hope.

But there was only just dark, flat, cold windows staring back at me.

Aubrey

Three days.

That's how long I'd been hiding under my blankets like a little girl hiding from a boogeyman. Except my boogeyman was real. He looked like a wet dream, smelled like sin, a grin that could drop any panties in the room.

And he'd managed to trick me into getting in mine.

I didn't know what to do. I didn't know who to turn to. *Noah* was my best friend. *He* was the one I would have called straight away. He would have come over, wrapped me up in one of his warm, solid hugs and let me cry out everything. He would have threatened the asshole who'd broken my heart with a lifetime of pain, made me laugh, fed me Murphy's caramelized brown bread ice cream and given me hope that things were going to be okay.

Except the one who'd betrayed me was him.

I kept hoping I'd wake up and it would all be some awful dream. But here I was, three days later, still pretending to be a burrito in my duvet like a dang toddler.

I fucking hated him. I hated his lies and his secrets. I hated that he risked our friendship for one night of sex. I hated the way my traitorous body heated up every time the memories from that night stole over me—his lips on my skin, eyes watching me from between my legs, the *feel* of him filling me. I hated that every single fond memory of Ireland had him in it, because they were all tainted now. He'd spoiled all of it. Ruined me.

But the part that I hated most of all…is that I didn't hate him at all.

From under the covers, I peeked at the TV. I'd turned on the news simply to find out the date and the day of the week.

I'd hidden my phone from myself. I was worried I'd call or text Noah without even thinking about it. Like I usually did when I found a funny picture or saw something awesome. I'd snap pictures and send them or send him good morning memes with some stupid *coffee is my life* quote attached. I'd send him short clips of what I was doing, pictures of food I'd cooked or ordered, bits of shows I was watching.

I didn't realize how much of the fabric of my life he'd woven himself into. Until he'd been ripped out of it.

That, and I'd not heard a peep from him.

After I'd missed the first day of work, I thought he might reach out. Use work as an excuse to see if I was okay, when I'd come in…

Then the second day dragggggged past.

And here we are. Day three.

Nothing. No calls, no texts, no fucking smoke signals. I might as well have dropped off the face of the earth for all he seemed to care.

It left me teetering between screaming at the face of my silent screen and crying into my pillow with the heartless bit of plastic clutched to my chest.

Hence, the phone was banished to the depths of my fridge, jammed between the wilting cabbage and half bottle of HP brown sauce.

"It would seem that that anonymous Irish Lottery we all heard about circling the internet found its winner," one news anchor said to another.

I choked on my inhale.

The blonde news anchor laughed before pouting. "It wasn't

me. Oh, man, though do I wish it had been!" She smiled brightly at the camera.

The male news anchor glanced at her. "And what was your fantasy, Carol?"

"That's none of your business, Tom," she said brightly with an edge to her voice that said she'd cut him if he kept pushing. "I can say that I bet hundreds of thousands of women are sobbing that they lost. But to that lucky winner out there," she said, looking into the camera like she could see into my soul, "enjoy yourself!"

I was going to be sick.

I lunged for the remote, cussing when I dropped it, fumbling with it like a hot potato before finally turning it off. The black screen mocked me. The silence swelled up around me, reminding me of how utterly alone I was.

Oh, I'd enjoyed myself. But that one incredible night, that one ultimate fantasy had cost me my best friend.

Aubrey

The knock at the door startled me. I jerked my head up off the couch pillow where I'd fallen asleep. I wiped at the crusted tears in the corners of my eyes.

Was I dreaming that knock?

It sounded again.

My heart leapt in my chest. *Noah.*

"Just a minute," I called out. I jumped off the couch in my ugly grey sweats and old faded tee shirt and hurried to the bathroom to splash water on my face. I caught sight of myself in the mirror. Dear God. I winced at the sight of me. I was going to need more than a little water. I grabbed my hairbrush and pulled my messy hair into a bun on my head. Mascara. I grabbed the wand and—

The knock came again. Shit. No time. This bare face was going to have to do. Besides, Noah had seen me without any makeup on about a million times.

I raced to the door, my heart pounding a million miles in my chest, already imagining him on my doorstep with a lamb kebab, hold the onions, extra hot sauce, as a peace offering, begging me to let him talk the second the door flew open.

Even though I wanted to slam the door in his face, I'd let him come in. I'd hear his apology and my heart would fill even though my features would stay stony. Because it was Noah.

It was *Noah*.

The only person I couldn't live without.

I unlocked the door and threw it open.

It wasn't Noah.

Candace's pretty face stared back at me. My heart slipped into my shoes. She didn't give me a chance to react before pushing into my apartment.

"Sure, come in, I guess," I muttered and closed the door behind us.

"Girl, you look awful."

I turned to face her. She was standing right where I'd stood in that sexy white lingerie the night the men had come over. I swallowed hard at the memory as Candace gave me an up and down look.

Of course I looked awful—I'd been hiding in bed for days. I don't think I'd showered since...

I crossed my arms protectively across my belly and shrugged as nonchalantly as I could. "I'm...sick." I let out a weak fake cough into my hand.

Her eyes narrowed, her magenta painted lips pursed. She shifted her weight to her right hip and planted her fist there. I wasn't fooling her for a second. "Heart*sick*, you mean?"

Oh fuck. She knew. Noah had told her. I couldn't form words. How dare he tell *anyone* about...about...

"You two are terrible at hiding your business," she said, walking over to my couch and taking a seat.

I followed her automatically, my limbs all numb.

"I don't know what you're talking about," I managed to say.

Candace lifted a hand. "I'm not going to say anything to anyone else, promise. I came over to make sure you were okay."

I nodded, feeling a bit of relief at her promise. "Thanks, Candace. You're a good friend." Tears stung in my eyes and I blinked them back while sucking in a deep, pained breath.

"Oh, honey," she said, pulling me into a hug.

I melted into her arms, feeling like maybe I wasn't so alone.

"Amiga?" she said.

"Yeah?"

"You really need to take a shower."

A half hour later, clean, dry and wearing fresh clothing, I sat across my little dining table from Candace. She had ordered Thai takeout delivery for two while I was in the shower after she'd discovered I had nothing in my fridge.

Candace had thrown open some windows, folded up my duvet and pillows that had been sprawled over the couch, thrown away the Tayto crisps and Snack bar wrappers littered around the room and lit a spiced mimosa and orange scented candle. These little things made my heart warm.

She'd also handed me my phone with a strange look. I thought she might have questioned my sanity but she just nodded and said, "When I left my asshole cheating bastard boyfriend, I rolled mine up in socks and stuck it in the dryer for a week."

Now the apartment smelled like fragrant spicy curry and coconut rice, steam rising up from the open takeaway containers as I spooned food onto my plate, mouth salivating, stomach rumbling. This would be the first real meal I'd had in days.

We ate in silence for a while until my burning curiosity got the better of my hunger.

Candace paused, a bite of red curry chicken halfway to her mouth as she stared at me over her perfectly held chopsticks. "I knew something was up because of Noah," she said.

I stiffened, the piece of baby corn crushed between my molars.

Noah was our boss. Well, her boss, anyway. I was as good as fired, I was sure. Or he could have assumed I quit. It was unprofessional of me not to show up at work, but, hello? Extenuating circumstances. That was totally unprofessional for him to spill our business. I could go over there right now and walk right up to that tall, handsome asshole and give him a piece of my mind.

"Don't blow an artery, he didn't *say* anything," Candace said, before she popped the bite in her mouth and chewed thoughtfully. While I waited for her to clarify, I set down my fork—appetite gone—and tried to slow my rapidly beating heart.

She swallowed. "He wouldn't talk about it, but I could tell he was miserable."

"He's miserable?" I wanted to rejoice in his misery, but I couldn't. It hurt me to know he was miserable. It also shattered any thought I had that I was the only one suffering.

Did he actually feel hurt because he knew he'd screwed up and lost me as a friend or…more?

"Gone is funny, happy Noah. All that's left is a grouchy, broody, angry shell of a man." Candace shook her head. "Brooding really doesn't work with him. Noah's too…boy next door, too wholesome Irish lad. Danny O'Donaghue, on the other hand…" Her eyes went all gooey as she mumbled on in Portuguese. I caught the words *so sexy* and *suck chocolate off his*—

"Candace." I snapped my fingers in front of her face. "Focus."

"Oh, right." She grabbed her unopened soda and pressed the condensing can to her neck. "The only reason Noah is ever this way is over you."

"Me?" I blinked.

Candace gave me a look. "I can tell you all of the five times over the last four years you guys have actually fought. One, the first summer when you'd introduced him to Sean and they'd almost gotten into a fist fight out the back of Bernard Shaw and almost took out the pizza cart. Two, that time you guys…"

As she continued to detail fights I'd totally forgotten about, my eyes widened.

"So, you see, amiga," she finished with, "every single time Noah's turned into a broody asshat has been when you and he are fighting."

"I—I didn't know," was all I could say.

"Of course you didn't know. Because by the time you next see each other, you've forgiven him and he's back to being Noah. But when you didn't show up for work at all I knew it was *bad*."

I nodded. Fair enough. It wouldn't have taken a genius to piece these things together.

"You want to talk about it?" Candace asked.

I shook my head.

"Sure?"

I nodded.

She lifted an eyebrow. "A problem shared…"

I let out a long sigh. Truth was, I was desperate to talk to someone. "We…we were intimate."

"Hah!" Candace slapped the table, startling me. "Finally."

I winced. Finally. Finally, I slept with the best friend everyone already thought I was sleeping with and it ended up with my heart being ripped into pieces.

"I take it you and Sean are over," Candace said.

I nodded, thankful that Candace hadn't made the assumption that I'd cheated.

"So, you and Hottie McBartender," she let out a wistful sigh. "Tell me details. No, wait! I don't want to know. Shit. Yes, I do." She leaned over the table, her eyes widening. "Was it amazing?"

Was it? It was mind-blowing, earthshattering…and heartbreaking. I let out a shaky breath and nodded. "It was…epic."

Candace let out a squeal which faded as she spotted my face. "So…the problem is?"

"He lied to me." It was about as close as I could get to the truth without violating the agreement I'd signed.

"About what?" she asked.

I shook my head. "Does it matter? He lied about something important. He hurt me. End of story." Feeling broken again, I knew my shoulders were sagging and I shoved the food around on my plate while blinking back tears. I'd cried more in the last couple days than I had my whole life leading up to now, I was pretty sure.

"Amiga," Candace said slowly, "when has Noah ever done anything without the best of intentions?"

I blinked at her, opened my mouth and closed it. I hated that she was right. As lost in my anger and pain as I'd been these last few days, I'd lost sight of the fact that I knew Noah. He was a good man with a good heart.

Even when it came to women? A voice inside me argued.

Even when it came to women. He might have been a player, but he had always been clear about what he offered. Just one night.

But with me… I…I didn't know what he was offering.

Candace nodded at me over our forgotten Thai. "We will always hurt the ones we love. It comes with letting people so close they can see our vulnerable underbelly. The only question is whether Noah is worth forgiving."

Could I forgive Noah? Could I forgive his lies? That he slept with me while pretending to be a stranger? Even now the burn of remembering the betrayal still raged in my heart.

I shook my head. "I don't know. Even if I could forgive him…" I trailed off.

"You guys have been circling each other for years, amiga. And now that something *more* has happened…why can't it *be* more?"

"He's too much of a player," I said, the words bursting out of me.

She frowned and leaned forward. When she spoke, her voice was staccato. "Name one woman he's gone home with since you've known him."

I thought about it, running through the last four years in my head.

Candace watched me, her dark eyes serious, her food forgotten.

Noah worked at the bar five or six nights of the week. He'd always taken me home, then texted me several times afterwards. He wouldn't have done that if he was lying next to someone else. I thought about the times we'd gone out together on his days off, the times he'd been slipped numbers by women on the sly. He'd often either ignored them or we'd had an *I can't believe the nerve of her* session or he'd make a joke. He always threw the numbers away in front of me.

I couldn't think of a single time he'd told me he had someone coming over or that he was going home with someone. We were good enough friends that he'd tell me, I was sure of that. Even if he'd been keeping it on the down low, I'd know. I mean, we spent all our time in almost constant contact. We texted first thing in the morning every day and last thing at night, too. There was no way he was texting me with a naked woman in his bed.

But tales of his conquests and the hordes of women that he'd dropped who were still chasing him were practically legends in The Jar. There were a ton of women who came there just to drink and stare at him, or who would flirt with him, or try to give him their numbers.

I'd heard all about the God of Thunder and about how he could make a woman forget herself. My cheeks stung. Oh boy, could he make a woman forget herself. That night he'd made me into a totally different person: some weak, knee-trembling mess of a human being who couldn't speak or think straight, much less remember my name.

Candace was still waiting for my answer.

"Um." I shifted in my chair. "I can't think of any."

"That's because…" Candace paused for dramatic effect, "…there haven't been any. Not since he met you."

I took a moment to assimilate this. She was right, but it sounded wrong. Was there really not one single night he'd taken someone home or gone home with them? Maybe I'd just forgotten…

"Okay, fine," I said. "So he's a reformed player. Whatever. Or he's just good at hiding it. But it doesn't change the fact that he's too hot for me."

"What?"

"He's so incredibly good-looking and could have any woman. Why would he even look twice at me?"

"*What?*"

"Women throw themselves at him all the time. I couldn't be with someone who was that beautiful. I'd be too stressed, too worried all the time." I was on a roll now. "I'd be jealous and unhappy knowing that I would have to compete with other women for his attention for the rest of my life. And what happens when I age and these…" I waved at my boobs, "…droop, or this…" I waved at my face, "…wrinkles? Men age like a fine wine. Women, we just get old." I shook my head. "No. I couldn't do it. I could never be with Noah. We could never work."

Candace stared at me for one long moment. She knocked back her head and let out a laugh, her palm slapping the table.

I blinked at her thinking she'd gone mad.

"That, amiga…" she wiped a tear from her eye, "…is the most ridiculous thing I've *ever* heard."

"It's true," I whined.

"Let me tell you something I've had to learn the hard way. Beauty is over-fucking-rated."

I stared at her. Now she really had gone mad.

"Trust me, I know. What? You're thinking of all those idiots staring at me all the time? I would trade all of this," she waved her hand over her youthful exotic face, her curvy body, "for just one man—one good-hearted man—who looked at me like I was his world. The way that Noah looks at you."

I sucked in a breath. Noah looked at me as if I was his world?

"When men look at beautiful things," Candace continued, "they are looking with their eyes, amiga. It's fickle, it fades, and there will always be another pretty young thing for the eyes to be temporarily distracted by. But when a man is in love, he sees who you are. That is real. That won't fade. And there is no beauty, nothing that is shiny or glittery enough, that can compare to what he sees when he looks at you with his *heart*."

I felt like she'd slapped me. I felt like my whole world was tilting on an axis, previous beliefs crumbling and falling apart like rotten wood. Pieces that I somehow didn't want to let go of. I shook my head, my hair falling around my face.

Candace leaned in. "Do you want to know what I think?"

No. I couldn't survive another truth bomb like that.

She kept talking anyway. "I think you're scared. Terrified. Because what you and Noah could have is so real, so fucking...*epic*, amiga, that it has the power to end you. So you make excuses—*he's too hot, he's a player, wahhh*—to avoid confronting what you feel in there." She pointed at my chest.

I pressed at my heart, shielding it with my hands, as if I could hide it from her. She already saw too much, this tiny firecracker of a woman.

Her words were like bullets punching through my armor. *So*

real. So…epic. It has the power to end you.

Even after one night of passion, after one lie, I had been ended by him.

Oh, shit. I… I glanced up at Candace, the realization stuck in my throat. *I…*

Candace nodded. "You love him, amiga."

I love Noah.

I'd always loved Noah.

I fell in love with him from the first laughter he'd so easily drawn from me the night that Sean stood me up. But I'd shied away from those feelings because I questioned my worth. I wasn't airbrushed or tall and rail-thin like those supermodels in magazines. I wasn't beautiful enough for a man like Noah. So instead of giving my heart what it wanted, I chose the safe option. Sean. The man I liked but whose feelings I could keep controlled, corralled into a safe, regulated box. So when it ended—like it had ended—I walked away, heart intact.

Oh, fuck.

I was in love with my best friend.

I was so fucked.

There was no way in hell I could ever go back to being friends with Noah, not with this realization beaming from my soul like a beacon, shining a new light over everything I did or said in front of him. Even if we could move on from this…

I shrugged, trying to emulate the apathy I wished I felt. Apathy didn't hurt like this did. "So I—" I choked on the word *love*, "have feelings for Noah. So what?"

Candace stared at me. She reached out between the forgotten Thai food containers and grabbed my hand, squeezing it. "You want to know the reason why he hasn't gone home with a woman in four years? Why he's a *reformed* player?"

I nodded.

"You."

"Me?"

She gave a rueful smile. "He's been in love with you since day one."

Noah. In love with me. No…

No?

Yes, Aubrey.

My heart began to slam in my chest.

All the nights Noah drove me home even though I was out of his way, refusing to drive away until I was safely inside.

The nights we stayed up until dawn, talking, laughing.

The way he kept me right into his side when we went to the crowded Electric Picnic festival. Rubbing my foot that time I'd cramped up on a hike in Glendalough.

The fact that he never liked Sean.

That he risked a massive fine by paying me cash under the

table when my student visa ran out.

Every step of the way he'd been an amazing friend to me. More than a friend.

He'd almost kissed me in the car that night. I ran. I'd kept him at arm's length like I'd been doing this whole time.

That night we spent together, he hadn't used me, he'd worshiped me. He didn't fuck me, he made love to me.

Maybe the lottery prize night wasn't the betrayal I thought it was.

I hadn't heard him out. I hadn't given him—my best friend in the whole wide world—a chance to explain himself. I could hear the echo of his voice I my head, those desperate words, *Aubrey, please, let me explain.*

I'd accused him of orchestrating the whole thing. Told him to get out rather than give him a chance to tell me his side. I'd been so wrapped up in how I felt and what was going on in my head. So determined to believe the worst in him. So determined to feel betrayed.

He got too close. He got under my skin. Showed me what we could be like. And I freaked. I used it as another reason to push him away.

Oh, fuck.

Now it was too late. He hadn't called since. He hadn't tried to come and see me to explain.

I stared at my silent phone now sitting on the edge of the table.

You haven't called him either.

"Oh, shit," I said, letting out a long breath, thinking of the mess we'd both made of this.

"Oh, shit," Candace agreed with a firm nod.

Noah

It was done. The surgery was booked and paid for. With the money from the lottery, plus the money we'd raised during Aubrey's fundraiser, we just about covered it.

The money had come so easily, yet now it was spent. Truth be told, I didn't miss a penny of it. I was actually glad it was gone. It felt like this ugly thing that tied me to a painful moment in my life had suddenly lost its power.

After I'd gotten off the phone to schedule the surgery, I'd had that moment of elation, an absolute thrill that everything was going to be okay. I felt like I could breathe again. I'd hit the instant dial on my phone before I knew what I was doing.

Calling Aubrey.

Except Aubrey wasn't talking to me anymore.

I hit cancel on the call before it connected, feeling like a knife had sliced through my heart. The one person I wanted to share this good news with, I had lost. Due to my own stupidity. I heard my phone creak as my hand curled around it in a fist, releasing it before I broke the damn thing.

Aubrey had been the inspiration behind the lottery idea, the whole reason that my ma was going to survive past next Christmas, and the whole reason I'd fucked things up so badly with her that I hadn't heard from her in days. The irony wasn't lost on me.

I missed her desperately. Every time the door opened at The Jar, my head snapped up, expecting her to waltz right in.

She hadn't.

Every time my phone beeped, I leapt to unlock the message, praying it'd be her, telling me she was ready to hear me out.

She hadn't.

Every second that went by was agony, like I was walking around with my chest torn open, bleeding out with every painful heartbeat. Because every second felt like she was moving further and further away. It was becoming clearer and clearer that I had lost her.

Really lost her.

Every time I'd gone to call her, I'd talked myself out of it. What would I say? What fecking excuse did I have that she would accept? If she was ready to hear me, she'd reach out to me, right?

Every night I closed down the bar without her; the space I loved, the place that'd felt like a second home, felt vacant. Like a stranger. I realized that it'd been Aubrey who had given The Jar its heart. Without it, the bar was just an empty shell of wood and glass.

Every night like a fucking eejit, I drove to her apartment. The silence of my car echoing in my ears. As I pulled up outside her building, I prayed that this time, this night, she would have left a light on. A sign that there was still hope.

She didn't.

I pushed open the front door of my childhood home—Ma never locked her damn front door, she was too used to growing up in the countryside—and caught sight of my ma in her chair, resting as she read a book.

She glanced up at me and her eyes twinkled. "Oh, would you look at that. It's my third favorite son."

I let out a laugh, my heartache temporarily relieved by her smile, lifted the paper carry bag I'd brought with me and shook it. "You might want to reconsider my ranking, Ma."

Her eyes widened and she sniffed the air. "Oh, is that…a

cheese toastie I smell?"

"From Grogan's. Picked it up on my way so it's still warm." I covered the distance between us and offered her the bag, the contents giving off the most delectable scent of melted cheddar.

My ma let out a squeal as she snatched the bag off me, managing to look like a child in that moment.

My heart squeezed.

"I take it back," she said, ripping open the bag in her lap and shooting me a loving look that made me feel like I was seven again. "You're at least my second favorite."

"Jaysus, Ma, wait a sec. You'll get it all over ye." I hurried to the kitchen and grabbed one of the mismatched plates from the cupboard and paper towels. You can't eat a cheese toastie from Grogan's without a roll of them. I returned to find she'd already disemboweled the paper and had taken a giant bite out of half of the cut sandwich, bacon grease running down her fingers, cheese oozing from the crust onto her lap.

"Ma!" I eyed the cheese pooling dangerously on the shredded paper wrapping, threatening to flood her skirt with oil. In one swift movement, I'd lifted the entire paper plus other half sandwich and slid the plate under it.

She gave me a closed-mouth grin as she chewed.

I rolled my eyes. "What would ye do without me?" I fell into the chair next to hers.

She let out a very unladylike snort. "I'd have fewer grey hairs, that's for sure." But the look she shot me was filled with affection.

"Ah, come on," I said. "Most of those grey hairs come from Eoin."

She popped the last of her toastie half into her mouth, the crunch of fried bread between her teeth.

"Damn, that does look good." I reached out to grab the other half.

"Mine." She slapped the back of my hand, leaving cheesy fingerprints on me.

"Aw, come on. Just a bite."

"I know your bites, Noah Michael O'Sullivan. Half my sandwich will be gone."

"A tiny bite?"

My ma lifted her eyebrow at me. "I raised you, boy. You don't do anything *tiny*."

I grunted and sank back into my chair, a small smile at my lips.

"So," my ma said, eyeing me out of the corner of her eye, "why are you here?"

I shifted in my chair under the weight of her stare. "Can't a son just come over to see his ma and bring her a toastie?"

"A son can. But that's not what's happening here." She circled a greasy finger around.

"Oh, ye of little faith."

"I'm your ma, boy. I know when you've got something weighing on ye." She took another bite of her toastie and waited for me to speak.

"Alright then," I said, feeling a grin overtaking my face. "Don't plan anything for August fifth."

Her eyebrow popped up. "Am I gonna need a dress?"

"What?"

"Mother of the groom dresses are all so ugly. So unflattering."

"*What?*"

"And those stupid strappy shoes that are all in fashion pinch tighter than a nun's assh—"

"*Ma!* What are you talking about?"

"No summer wedding?"

I blinked at her.

She shot me a look. "You didn't finally get that girl of yours to dump her fiancé and marry you instead?"

Bitterness flooded my mouth. I'd have to tell Ma that I'd fucked things up irreparably with Aubrey, but the good news came first. I would not spoil this moment for her. "No," I said through gritted teeth.

My ma chuckled her tongue. "I didn't think I raised an eejit, but sure three out of four ain't bad."

I forced a smile, trying to get the conversation back on track. The conversation about Aubrey had to wait. Or happen…never. "That surgery you need, I scheduled it."

"In me hoop, you did. We can't afford it," she said.

"It's already paid for. I paid for it. *We* paid for it," I corrected, not wanting to take all the glory. "Eoin, Darren, Michael, we all covered it."

I'd asked my brothers if they wanted to be here to tell Ma, but they'd all told me that it was my idea so I should tell her myself. It'd be a more civilized conversation, Michael had said whilst side-eyeing Eoin. He'd earned a slap on the back of the head for that.

I think they also didn't know what to do around me or what to say. They were all worried about me, all of them taking turns to drop by the bar because they were "just passing through." Liars. They were never "just passing by." I was on their bloody roster. They knew something went wrong between Aubrey and me that night, but I hadn't given them any details. I couldn't bring myself to talk about it. Or that night.

I'm sure they thought I needed some time alone with Ma.

My ma was now staring at me, remnants of her toastie all but forgotten on the plate.

In all my life, I don't think I'd ever rendered her speechless. "Surprise," I said weakly.

"You selling guns?" she demanded, brows furrowing.

"What? No!"

"Running drugs for the Irish Kings?" she said, referencing one of the most notorious gangs in Ireland.

"Jaysus, Ma!"

"Then how the feck do four lads raise almost a feckin' quarter of a feckin' million euros?"

I don't think I'd ever heard my ma say so many fecks in a row in my whole life. I froze. "It doesn't matter how. It's paid for."

"Me bollocks, it doesn't. I didn't raise my boys to steal, lie or cheat."

I let out a sigh. Time for a little white lie. Or four. "We didn't steal, lie or cheat. We all just pitched in, got loans. I refinanced my bar, Darren took a mortgage out on his shop, we all know Michael's been hoarding away money since the day he could count cents, Eoin signed a big sponsorship deal. Relax, Ma. We got this."

She eyed me for a moment as if to determine whether I was trying to pull the wool over her eyes.

I prayed that she wouldn't sniff out the lies. I hated keeping the truth from her. But it was for her benefit, I reasoned to myself.

Finally, my ma blinked. "You...raised all that money."

I nodded, still too scared to speak in case I blurted out the truth of how we did it.

"For me?"

"It's the least we could do for our second favorite ma."

For a moment, she just stared at me.

It started with a chin wobble.

Then her eyes misted over. A choking noise came from her throat, and I realized she was trying to say my name. And failing.

That's when my solid as a rock ma, the centerpiece of our family, the woman who stepped up without shedding a tear and became both parents when our deadbeat father left us, broke down.

My heart squeezed so hard I felt the sting in my own eyes. I fell to my knees in front of my sobbing ma, pulled the plate off her lap and wrapped her in a hug, not caring if she got cheese grease all over me.

"How did I ever—I—you..." she kept muttering between huge gulps of air.

"You're welcome," I whispered. In that moment, I stopped cursing the lottery and the fallout between Aubrey and me. And just enjoyed being with the only other woman in my life that I loved. Getting to keep one out of two ain't bad, I supposed dryly to myself.

My ma let out a cough, a sniff and pulled herself back, dabbing at her damp cheeks. "Well then," she said with a nod. But her eyes were still glittering with emotion.

"Well then," I said with an awkward smile, still kneeling before her, trying to pretend like this was just normal Ma and son bonding behavior.

"I raised you boys well." She patted my cheek. "One day, you're going to make that Aubrey the happiest woman in the world."

And from the heavens to the depth of hell, my heart crashed and burned.

There was no force in the universe that could have prevented the surge of emotions from rising up and crashing out all over my face.

"Oh no," my ma said in a quiet voice.

I shoved myself up from the floor, slumping back into the chair I'd occupied before.

"What happened?"

"Don't want to talk about it," I said through gritted teeth.

There was a silence. My ma picked up the plate and carefully ate the rest of her toastie, one nibble at a time, all the while staring at me with narrowed eyes. This was my ma's carefully honed strategy to get information out of us boys. Silence. Silence that squeezed you till you popped. Catholic priests could learn a thing or two from her about how to get you to confess.

And it was working. I could feel that pressure building up in me like a soda someone had shaken.

"Stop lookin' at me like that," I muttered, crossing my arms over my chest, feeling my bottom lip stick out in a pout. I didn't want to say it out loud. If I said it out loud, it'd make it real.

Her brows shot up into her hair. "That bad, huh?"

I let out a long groan, shoving my hands over my face. Maybe I did want to talk about it. Maybe I wanted to share my hurt. For Ma to make it better with soft hands that smelled like lavender laundry soap and kisses that had magical boo-boo fixing powers.

"I hurt her," I blurted out. "We were…intimate and I messed up." My heart sank into my toes at finally admitting to myself what I'd done. "I've lost her."

"Aubrey could never be lost to you."

I nodded, feeling a wail rising up through my lungs. "She is. She won't talk to me. She won't forgive me. Ever."

I withered with shame under Ma's cool stare. I knew she loved Aubrey, maybe as much as I did. I knew she'd pinned her hopes on us getting together. Even when I'd told her that Aubrey had gotten engaged to Sean, she'd shrugged and said in a knowing tone, *"What's for ye, won't pass ye,"* that old Irish saying.

"How many sunflowers have you sent her?" she asked. Sunflowers were Aubrey's favorite.

I blinked. "None."

"Boxes of those Butlers champagne truffles she loves?"

"No."

"Marching a band up and down her street playing her favorite songs and holding up a large sign saying 'I'm sorry I'm such a feckin' eejit'???"

I winced.

"Well, what have you tried?"

"I…tried talking to her…apologizing…" Actually, now that I think about it, did I actually *say* the words *I'm sorry*?

"Fifty times?" my ma asked.

"Um…once?"

"Jaysus, Mary and Joseph." My ma looked up to the heavens. "Lord forgive me, I *have* raised a fecking eejit."

"*Ma!*"

She glared at me. "Of course she won't forgive you, you haven't feckin' tried."

"I was giving her space to cool off," I argued. "She didn't want to hear me out. She told me to get out."

"And then?"

"And then… she never called." If Aubrey didn't want to talk to me, wasn't I supposed to leave her alone until she came to me? Wasn't this me respecting her wishes? I mean, when I told my brothers to fuck off, they left me alone. They knew I'd go to them when I was ready to hash that shite out, usually through a couple of decent punches while rolling around in the dirt, then heading to the pub for a pint afterwards.

Like with Darren. I had lost my fucking mind when he'd admitted that he'd rigged the lottery after finding Aubrey had entered when he was fixing her laptop. I'd punched him in the nose before Eoin and Michael had separated us and then stormed off. Days later, I'd showed up at his mechanic shop for round two. We'd gone to the pub afterwards and he admitted he thought it'd be the ticket to pushing us clueless eejits together.

Fuck me, women were confusing.

Ma snorted. "Men," she mumbled under her breath. "Have I taught you nothing about women?"

"Obviously not," I muttered.

Ma sighed. "Ye boys never do until someone smacks you in the nose with it. Son," she said, her voice growing steady, "when you fuck up with Aubrey, which you're going to do again and again, you give her some space so she can cool off and you have time to figure out what you have to do to prove to her that you're truly sorry."

"But I am. Truly."

Ma rolled her eyes. "Words mean shite without actions to back them up. Prove to her that you're actually sorry and not just talking shite out your hoop. You need to grovel."

"Okay."

"Like, international gold medal-winning groveling."

"Fine."

"Forget your pride, shove your dignity in a blender and—"

"Okay, I got it already."

"And you better do it soon because I want grandbabies."

"*Ma!*"

She grabbed my hands in hers. "I've been watching you two for the last four years. Even a blind person could see that you're mad for her. And she is for you."

Hope pricked at my soul. Maybe my ma was right.

"Tell her the truth," my ma continued. "Tell her how you feel about her. Be open and honest. Promise her you'll be the man she deserves."

My stomach tightened.

The man she deserved.

Aubrey deserved so much.

So much more than Sean.

So much more…than me.

"That's just it, Ma," I said in a whisper. "I'm not the man she deserves."

And there, laid bare, was the real reason why I'd hung up before the call connected these last few days. Why I stayed in that feckin' car staring at her windows instead of banging down her door. Why I'd left her apartment that night without a fight.

She deserved better than me.

"Bollocks," Ma said.

"I'm *not* good enough for her," I said, meaning every word.

"I'm just a bartender who hurt her. I don't have a degree or a fancy job. I can't buy her a big house or take her travelling. The life I offer her isn't enough." I was just a pretty face and a well-kept body that women liked to ride. Once.

The words didn't even sting. They were the simple, honest truth. She'd dated Sean, an up-and-coming lawyer with sophistication and family money, and even *he* wasn't good enough for her.

"Noah, a man doesn't become worthy of a woman because of *what* he is or what he can *buy* her. He becomes worthy because of *how he treats her.*"

I blinked, staring at my ma like I'd only just realized she was human. Like she'd been through her own life of love and loss. She wasn't just my ma, but a grown woman.

Despite my ma's words, fear still crept in. If I tried and failed, then all would be lost. "What if she refuses to listen to me?"

"Even if she slams her door in your face, you can bet she's on the other side of it, hurting and listening. Confess your heart to her anyway."

"And if she doesn't open the door?"

"Go back the next day and the next and the next until she does. And if that doesn't work, I know a great marching band."

For the first time since that night, a light came on inside me.

I just had to treat Aubrey better than anyone would or could ever treat her. And that didn't necessarily mean buying her things. God, how stupid was I? Aubrey had never been a materialistic person anyway. She was a simple girl at heart with simple tastes.

Her favorite things to do were to sit in a candlelit corner of Blackbird with me, a pint and a game of Connect 4. Or walking around Glendalough Lake as I taught her to skip stones. Or catching a free Riff Raff comedy gig at the Chelsea Drugstore and laughing until we collapsed into tears. Or eating kebabs with me on the floor of her living room.

Suddenly, all the things I had to tell Aubrey rose to a shout inside me, impatient from being repressed for so many years. All I needed to do was figure out how to tell her that I was a feckin' eejit, but I was *her* eejit. I would spend the rest of my life making her fall in love with me if she just gave me a chance.

Noah

A man doesn't become worthy of a woman because of what he is, he becomes worthy because of how he treats her.

With my mother's words ringing in my ears, I walked up the stairs to Aubrey's front door, a neighbor walking out, having let me in downstairs. Every step felt like my feet were growing heavier and heavier.

I wanted to run. Run as far away from this mess I'd made and this icky vulnerable feeling. But I kept walking. No matter how sick to my stomach I felt at the thought of her slamming the door in my face, I had to risk it. She was worth it.

Even if I had to pour my heart out to her front door like a fool. A fool in love.

Her door came into sight and I froze, blood draining from my limbs. Aubrey was hugging Sean. Now she was stepping aside and—and—letting him into her apartment.

Something ugly wormed through my gut, irritation hummed in my head. My fingernails dug into my palms and I swear I let out an actual growl.

No.

Sean could not say his piece first.

He did not deserve Aubrey.

He didn't love her like I loved her.

I would not let him sweep her out from underneath my feet. Again.

Channeling Eoin, I charged at the door, fists raising to pound it open.

I planted a hand on the door, stopping it from catching before it closed. I shoved it open, pushing myself into Aubrey's apartment.

I almost ran Aubrey over. She stumbled back a few steps, her eyes wide on me, her face paled. The hollow at the base of her neck bottomed out as she stared at me, her chest was rising and falling so hard.

I know. I was breaking all sorts of laws at that moment. Breaking and entering. Trespassing. Being a world-class eejit.

Whatever. I had lost my mind with jealousy. Sean had snatched Aubrey from me once. I'd be feckin' dammed if I let him do it again.

"You can't accept Sean back. You don't love him," I said.

Speaking of the knob-end, I could feel Sean staring at me. I ignored him, my focus only on Aubrey.

Her throat shifted up as she swallowed hard and she glanced between Sean and me.

Was she trying to make up her mind?

I kept going. This was my one shot at getting her back. "He doesn't make you happy. You deserve someone who makes you happy, someone who puts you first. And... And he doesn't love you."

"Noah," Sean had the nerve to say in that insufferable Dublin 4 accent.

"Shut up," I snarled at him. "Don't tell me you love her. Not as much as—" *Not as much as I do. I have more love for her in my pinky toe than in your whole feckin' soul. Say it, Noah.*

"Noah." This time it was Aubrey who spoke. "I think there's been a mistake."

"No. No mistake. I've made a ton of mistakes with you, fuck

knows, I have, but *this* is not a mistake. You deserve someone who loves you—who loves you more than their own life. And I…" *I am that man. Say it.* I let out a growl. "I fucked up. I know. And I had this whole apology worked out but I don't want to do it in front of *him*."

Sean cleared his throat. "Well, I'll just take my things and be on my way then."

"I…" Wait, he what?

Sean picked up a box by his feet that I hadn't noticed before. A box of odds and ends. A button-down shirt. A silk tie. A couple of books, a movie, a rain jacket. Things that someone might have left at their ex's place…and need to have returned.

With the box under one arm, Sean walked up to Aubrey and pressed a key into her outstretched palm. Her fingers closed around it. He leaned in and kissed her cheek, a quick kiss, a sign of courtesy.

She nodded at him.

Then without another word, he turned and walked towards the door, skirting around me to get out.

The door closed behind him with a click. For the first time since that night I'd made love to her, I was alone with Aubrey.

She stared at me.

"He wasn't here to ask for you back," I said dumbly.

She shook her head.

"He just came to pick up his stuff," I bumbled on. Ma was

right. I was a fecking eejit.

"Why are you here?" I could hear a tremor in her voice, could see the pain in her beautiful eyes.

All the words I had prepared to say flew out of my head.

Lord help me.

I was left dumb.

Wordless.

No ammunition left to fight for her.

Aubrey

I hated Noah.

Hated him for barging into my apartment. For accusing me of getting back with a man I didn't love.

As we stood wordless, just staring at each other, I hated him for the swollen silence. For stealing my breath when I looked at him. For making my heart ache just to feel him in the room.

I let out a huff when it was clear he wasn't going to speak, anger stacking like bricks around me like a shield. "We obviously have nothing to say to each other." I brushed past him, warmth sparking through my shoulder at his touch. *Stay strong, Aubrey.* "I think you should leave." I placed my hand on the door handle.

A warm hand covered mine.

"Please…"

His voice ruffled my hair, sending a shiver down my spine.

I tried to swallow down the rising knot of emotions. Failed. It was his hand. His hand on me that was cluttering my brain. Making me stupid.

I snatched my hand away from his, rubbing where he'd touched me with my other hand. But the heat wouldn't go.

"Please, look at me."

Fuck.

With feet like lead, I turned. Reminding myself how much he'd hurt me. Promising myself I wouldn't accept it even if he did apologize. Telling myself that he'd only hurt me again.

I was lost the second I stared into those eyes.

"I…I booked and paid for Ma's surgery," he said.

I smiled even though it felt like a crack spreading through dry earth. "I'm glad. She must have been over the moon."

"You know Ma. Giving me grief over spending so much money on her. Accusing me of running guns to pay for it."

"Sounds like her." I dropped my gaze, unable to keep looking at him. Perhaps it would be easier to forgive him if it had been guns that'd funded her surgery. Rather than my broken heart. "Well, thanks for coming around to tell me about it."

Noah didn't move. "The second it was done, the first thing I wanted to do was to call you. I did call. Then I hung up." His cheeks colored.

I gritted my teeth. "Well, we were friends for years. Calling me is just a habit. A habit you'll grow out of."

"No."

"No?"

"I'm not going to grow out of you."

"What?"

"Ah, feck, I'm doing this all wrong."

I could see the frustration in his eyes, like his words just weren't enough.

He inhaled and let it all out, a sudden sureness in his features. "I'm sorry."

I swallowed hard. "Go on."

"I should have told you about the lottery."

That we could agree on.

"I should have told you that it was me. I should have told you I wanted you to see me as more than a friend. Instead of hiding who I was under a mask, I should have told you I wanted to make love to *you*."

I sucked in a breath.

He moved towards me, his stare so intense that I felt like he might never let me go if he caught me. I backed up.

"But the thing I should have done most, Rey, was to tell you…"

My back pressed against the door and I could get away no more.

He leaned in. "The night we spent together wasn't just some fucking lottery prize. It was *real*. I know you felt it, too."

The ice that had formed around my heart began to thaw. "So what if you and I felt it?" I said, my voice all rough. "It's too late."

"Don't say that." His finger traced my cheek, his eyes dropping to my mouth.

I shook my head. His nearness was confusing me, making me stupid. "It is," I whispered. "Because I have to return to the US soon and we're going to lose each other anyway." It was a cruel joke played on us by the universe. We'd finally admitted what we were to each other only to be torn apart.

"Aubrey, you remember when we watched that movie? I can't remember the name, but it had that ending, that stupid ending, after the lovers were separated and I was like, wait, did he end up with her or not? And you said—"

"Where there is love, there is hope," I finished for him.

Noah smiled. "Where there is love, there is hope," he repeated. "Aubrey, I love you. I've always loved you. And it doesn't matter if you don't love me back, I have enough love for both of us. Enough hope for both of us."

Every word squeezed around my aching swollen heart. I loved him too. More than I could ever explain.

I wanted to tell him so. To speak. But…

He slid his hands around my jaw, until he held my face in his hands, looking at me as if I were his whole world.

And I knew right this second, I'd never doubt what he felt for me. I'd never question whether any other pretty glittery woman was beautiful enough to steal his attention. Because when Noah O'Sullivan looked at me, it was with his *heart*.

He leaned in and pressed his lips to mine.

His kiss was like a balm, soothing over the rough, wounded edges he had made. Stitching back the pieces of my heart.

We kissed for every second we spent apart.

We kissed for every minute we'd wasted, not kissing.

We kissed for all the years we hoped to have left kissing.

He pulled away, leaning his forehead against mine. "I wanted to kiss you so many times over the last four years."

"Why didn't you?"

"Sean. I thought you were happy with him. Your happiness meant more to me than my own. It still does. If you don't think I could make you happy, I'll walk away. If you tell me the only way to make you happy is to be your friend again, that's what I'll do and never ask for more. But…"

"But?"

"But I'm hoping you'll give me a chance to show you…if you let me…I will spend the rest of my life making you happy." He dropped to one knee, holding my hands in one of his.

"What are you doing?" I squealed.

"Marry me," he said. "Stay here. I don't care if you only want to be friends, I just need you in my life."

It was the sweetest thing anyone had ever offered to do for me.

"No."

His expression shifted from stunned to hurt, his hands falling from mine. "No?"

I kneeled down in front of him and took his hands. "I won't marry you so I can stay in Ireland. I'll marry you because I'm in love with you, Noah Michael O'Sullivan, my best friend. And I want to spend the rest of my life with you."

Noah blinked at me, saying nothing for so long I started to feel self-conscious.

"Say something," I begged.

"I must be dreaming."

"What?"

"I've dreamed about hearing you say those words for almost four years." His gaze held mine, piercing me right into my soul the very way he did when we were making love that night. That's what it was. Making love. The first three orgasms had been about pleasure. But with Noah, it was all love. Even when he was fucking me hard into the mattress. "Say it again," he whispered.

"Which part?" I said, suddenly shy.

"The part when you told me you're in love with me. You...love me?"

I laugh-cried. "Yes."

Suddenly, he was standing, pulling me up into those big strong arms I'd been missing so terribly. I found myself wishing we'd admitted our hearts long ago. I hated how much time we'd lost, how much pain we'd both suffered for no good reason.

"I missed you so much," he whispered into my hair as he squeezed me as tightly as he dared.

I tilted my head back to look up at him. "I missed you, too," I said.

His eyes ticked to my mouth before he lowered his lips to mine. This time his kiss wasn't gentle. It was raw and desperate. He growled, his teeth capturing my lower lip before he kissed me deeply. Our tongues met and danced and my heart pounded in my chest. I wanted him, I wanted him more than I ever thought possible. More than when he was just the masked Blue.

Our hands became frantic, roaming across each other, pulling off clothes, as if the last four years had been foreplay and we would both explode if he wasn't inside me right now. Like we'd been kept apart for years and we couldn't get enough.

This time, there would be no mask.

There would be no lottery. No winners. No secrets.

Just Aubrey. And Noah. And—

The front door banged, startling me. I tore my mouth off Noah's as I stared at the door.

"Leave it. We're not home," Noah whispered.

I giggled and pressed my lips to his again.

The door banged even louder. I let out a sigh into Noah's mouth. "It's probably Sean. He must have forgotten something."

Noah stilled, his shoulders sagging as if accepting that our much-anticipated reunion would need to be postponed. "Better go see what he wants and get it over with then." Noah kissed me hard, causing the lust to swirl around in my body. "I'll wait for you in the bedroom."

I giggled as he grabbed his shirt from the floor, sending me a wink over his shoulder as he disappeared into my bedroom.

I yanked my t-shirt on and walked to the door. "Coming, Sean." I swung open the door. "What did you for—?"

It wasn't Sean standing on my threshold. It was a man I didn't recognize. He was a bit older, maybe in his forties or fifties with a thick crop of dark hair. Was he wearing makeup? Behind him stood a man with a camera on his shoulder aimed right at my face.

"Tell the world about your lottery winner's night, Aubrey!" the reporter said in an overly excited voice.

"*What?*"

I felt every muscle in my body lock up. Shock rippled through me, my guts twisted like a python around prey. I'd been found out.

How the hell had they found me? This had to be a joke or something. These were some jokers sent by Darren. Or Eoin. Yeah, this is something they'd do. But deep down, I knew they wouldn't.

"You know…" the reporter said, "four hot Irishmen playing out your ultimate fantasy?"

"I—I don't know what you're talking about. I didn't win."

"Oh really?" Both the reporter's eyebrows creeping up a quarter inch, his disbelieving tone ringing in my ears. "Because we got a hold of the fantasy you emailed in. Tell me if this sounds familiar…*I just want someone to give me an orgasm.*"

I stumbled back as my whole world crashed down on me. My heart began to pound painfully fast in my chest. My face stung and I knew I was going bright red. A gleam of satisfaction lit the reporter's eyes and I knew my horrified, raw reaction had been caught on camera. No one watching this footage would have any doubt I had won and shared a night with four men.

"What's going on here?" Noah called from behind me. He must have come out from the bedroom, wondering why I was taking so long.

I wanted to melt into him, to run away from here and pray that I was imagining this nightmare. He appeared beside me, wrapping a protective arm around my shoulder and pulling me against him, his jaw tight. I curled into his side.

"Did you know your girlfriend slept with four men behind your back?"

Noah's expression turned murderous. "Leave her alone," he growled in a low primal voice. "Or I will fucking end you." I'd never heard him speak this way before. I'd never seen him this furious.

I caught the look of fear flashing across the reporter's face before Noah slammed the door shut. The light sound of the bolt sliding home didn't make me feel safe. Because the door wouldn't hold anything back. It was too late. The truth was going to be all over the news. That private night between the four of us, between Noah and me, out for the public to feast on. My private plea for an orgasm exposed for the world.

This couldn't be happening. How had they found me? How had they gotten a hold of my entry? I knew that there was no way the brothers had sold me out. Heck, Michael and Eoin had more to lose than I did if this became public knowledge.

Eoin could lose his spot on his rugby team, Michael could lose the hard-earned respect he had at his firm. They could lose everything if this got out to the mainstream public. And it would all be my fault, because somehow, my information was what had leaked. Or was it everything? Did this man know everything?

How could I ever leave the house again? How could I face anyone? Oh, God. How could I look at Ma again? I burned with shame. A sob escaped me.

Noah pulled me against his chest, wrapping both arms around me as if he could shield me from the world. He couldn't. "I swear I'll make this better."

I didn't believe him. He couldn't undo what had been done.

Nobody could.

Noah

Darren's shop smelled like motor oil and rubber, tasted like summers helping Darren rebuild old cars, and felt like a home away from home. I wasn't in the headspace to appreciate any of it. I was struggling to keep my fury in check. I stepped over the creeper Darren used to work under cars to stand before him.

"How the fuck did they find out about her?" My voice echoed off the shop walls.

Darren glanced up at me and told the young mechanic standing next to him to take a break.

The young lad scurried off, wide eyes.

I ignored his backward glances at me.

The look of heartbreak in Aubrey's eyes, the hollow expression that hadn't left her face since the reporter showed up outside her door, haunted me. I felt personally responsible. It should have been anonymous. I should have protected her from this. I'd failed.

Darren faced me once we were alone in the shop. "I'm sorry." The tight set to his lips told me he was tightly controlling his own rage.

"I don't want your sorries, I want to know how they found her."

"I'd only be guessing," Darren said, wiping his oily hands on a rag.

"Then guess," I said through gritted teeth.

"Someone hacked into the giveaway program, got her IP address attached to her entry and used that to track down her computer."

"Why didn't you protect her from being hacked?" I screamed at him.

Every part of Darren sagged, from his shoulders to the corners of his mouth.

I instantly felt like an asshole. But I couldn't stop. The woman

I loved was suffering. "This is your fault," I hissed. I felt my fists clench at my side. I'd fuck up the motherfucker that dug for this information and used it to hurt her. I'd kill them. All of them.

Darren raised his palms to face me. "I know you're pissed. I'm fucking pissed, too. But I'm not going to fight with you, you crazy bastard."

"*Fuck!*" I screamed out into the shop.

I turned on my heel and strode across the shop, ignoring Darren calling out for me. I began to beat on the bag Darren had hung back in a corner for quick lunch break workouts. He was quick to come hold the bag for me. With every pounding punch and kick, his whole body jolted. His jaw tightened as he leaned into the bag. I let it out, landing blow after blow after blow until my knuckles screamed and sweat dampened my shirt.

"I'm sorry," Darren repeated, rubbing the back of his hand over his damp forehead.

I shook my head. "It's not your fault."

"What can I do?" He gave me such a desperate look, one that mirrored how I felt.

"Nothing." My shoulders sagged as the truth hit me. Even I couldn't do a damn thing. "How come they didn't find out about us?" I asked, not really caring if we were outed too.

"I made sure the giveaway website was untraceable. We won't be exposed. Unless…"

Unless Aubrey outed us.

"She wouldn't," I growled. "Fuck you for even suggesting she would."

Darren lifted up his hands again in surrender. "Chill, bro. I know she wouldn't. But you know me, I wouldn't care if she did. I think it'd be better for her if we stood up next to her, but…"

But Eoin and Michael would lose everything.

I couldn't ask my brothers to do that.

Aubrey

They're calling her Easy A!

"Because her name is Aubrey," the blonde RTE news anchor said to the other, leaning in like she was revealing a joke. They both laughed even though it wasn't funny. At all. I wiggled deeper under the pile of blankets I was hiding in on the couch as I changed the channel.

"These guys were super smart, see, because they had masks on and no one knows their identity. It's not like she could call them again afterwards!" The two male BBC One newscasters broke out laughing.

The other guy piped up, "Man, how many times have you tried to kick a gal out the door after, only to have her show up at your place later?"

"Like when your wife is home?" the first guy said, clapping the other on the back.

I changed the channel.

"See, they had the right idea," an Ireland AM presenter said, while the other two men and lone woman leaned in subtly like they were waiting for the punchline. "Clever bastards got to sleep with an attractive woman and made money off it."

"Yeah, but who knows how else she paid them in return," the woman said, her waggling eyebrows revealing what she really meant.

The third presenter spoke up. "Yeah, a venereal disease!"

Their laughter made me sick to my stomach. I should stop watching, but I just couldn't. It was like watching a car crash. But…this was *my life* being torn apart before my eyes.

I changed the channel.

A frozen image of me in my doorway, red-faced, mouth open in shock, appeared on screen behind two female presenters. At least they didn't choose a still with Noah in it as well.

"…with the identity of the four men still unknown, the one feeling public backlash is Aubrey Campbell, identified as an American living in Dublin."

The second presenter. "And she should be; this is shameless and disgusting."

How many of these very women had sent in their own entries? Who had also tried for this prize and now sat up on their high horses talking me down?

"This will die down soon," Noah said, walking in and turning off the TV.

I stayed hidden under the blankets. I'd had to stay at Noah's place since the media was parked outside mine. I'd even received death threats, and a certain American religious group was picketing about how I was a loose woman and how God hated proud sinners like me. I hadn't left Noah's apartment in days because the last time I walked down the road to get milk at the local shops, I was given dirty looks. I was filmed by people's cell phones, held up in my face like I was some kind of celebrity in the middle of a breakdown. People shouted all manner of things at me, from calling me a whore to telling me to just kill myself. Strangers told me to kill myself. Because I'd won a prize and had a wonderful night of passion with four men. People thought I should die for that.

Maybe they were right. I mean, enough people say a thing, it must be true, right? I'd seen those words pour into my email, flood my social media, everything. I'd closed down all my accounts, I'd turned off my phone.

It felt like my life was over. Noah was my one faint ray of

sunshine in an otherwise dark place. The only thing keeping me going.

"Ignore them," he said, hunkering down before me. With gentle hands he moved the blankets away from my face, opening the viewing porthole I'd allowed myself. He ran his thumbs over my face and brushed back my sweaty hair. "The people who love you will support you."

I wasn't so sure. I hadn't seen Ma since all of this, but I knew there was no way she'd let me—a ruined, loose woman—marry her son. Why would she approve?

Noah leaned in and pressed his lips to mine.

I let him kiss me. For one moment I let myself forget the disaster that was my life and lose myself in his lips.

When he pulled away, I whimpered as the world caved in on me again.

"Are you going to come out of that blanket?" he asked softly.

I shook my head and tried to burrow myself deeper into my fort. Not that the fort could stop the world from laying siege on my life.

"Rey? At least come out and give me a proper hug before I head off to The Jar."

I let out a groan.

"Candace has been asking about you. She's worried."

I knew burrowing myself in blankets wasn't healthy. I was handling things badly. Time to put my big girl panties on.

There was no reason to let strangers dictate how I lived my life. I had to leave the damn house sometime. Right? And I couldn't let Noah keep supporting me without paying my own way.

"I think I want to do my shift tonight," I said softly in a voice that didn't even sound like me.

"Are you sure?"

"No...yes... I need to get out of the house. I need to earn my way—"

"I don't care about that."

"Noah," I said softly, "you can't keep housing me and feeding me forever while I hide out in your apartment."

Noah gave me a look that said, *I can.*

My heart warmed. If I hadn't fucking loved him enough before now... "I know you would," I said. "And I love you for it. But I am going to do a shift."

Noah studied me for one long moment, then nodded. "I'll be right there beside you, babe."

His words were tiny candles of hope. As long as Noah was by my side, I'd get through this. Right?

Twenty minutes later, after showering and feeling halfway human again, we were parking outside The Jar.

Noah had turned on one of our happy '80s music mixes during the car ride and had spent all of two minutes belting out the words to "Shook Me All Night Long" by AC/DC before giving up. I was barely listening, silent the whole way, too busy trying to talk myself out of having a breakdown.

The Jar would be safe, right? People there knew me. They were my friends.

"Not too late to turn around," Noah said.

I shook my head. "I'm okay." I shot Noah a smile that I didn't feel.

With Noah at my side, we walked into The Jar.

Candace spotted us and made a beeline right for me, ignoring the table she'd been standing at.

My first instinct was to turn and flee, but Noah's hand rested at my lower back, keeping me in place.

With a squeal, she rushed up and threw her arms around me. "You lucky bitch," she said in my ear before backing off and beaming at me.

Other staff members waved and smiled at me.

I breathed a sigh of relief. Maybe Noah was right. Maybe the people who mattered would support me. After all, why did I care what a bunch of strangers thought of me? It's not like they were living my life. They had no right to judge me. They sure as hell didn't know my story.

I made myself busy, waiting on tables with a smile plastered on my face that grew less fake and more real as the night went on. Noah would come over and check in on me every so often, making sure I was still okay, placing a hand on my back or pressing his lips to my forehead. It made me smile every time he did it.

As people came in, I noticed a few staring at me, but most didn't. A few people whispered as I passed. Most didn't.

That was enough to keep my chin up.

A loud noise at the door drew my attention as three young men burst in, obviously intoxicated. The guy I instinctively identified as the ringleader saw me and a grin spread across his face. He smacked his friends' chests, turning their attention to me. They all stumbled towards me.

I backed up a step, knowing this wasn't going to go well.

"You're that girl," the first one said, slurring his speech.

He was loud enough that heads began to turn towards me.

I swallowed hard, unable to find my voice to respond. Not that it made any difference.

The guy spread his arms out to the sides in a weak attempt to hit the pose Noah had in the picture they'd posted on the website for the lottery. "Me and my pals here," he said, looking from one to the other, "would love to give you an orgasm. All of us. I know you like that kind of thing, you know, being shared—"

I screamed as Noah hurtled across the bar, his whole weight behind the fist he threw at the ringleader's face. I heard and *felt* the crunch of bones as he connected.

"Noah, stop!" I screamed.

But he was on top of the guy, punches flying, shouting that he better fucking apologize to me if he wanted to walk away with *only* a broken nose.

The bar erupted into chaos.

Noah

In the holding cell, I sat on the edge of the uncomfortable cot and touched my lip. It was tender and swollen. My eyes jumped to my knuckles, which were busted…likely from smashing that asshole's nose. I could feel bruises forming along my ribs where his friends leapt in to help him.

I didn't give a damn about bruises. Or the fact that I was spending the night in the local Garda station. I'd done what I'd done and I'd done it to protect Aubrey. Maybe those guys were just hot air. But what the fuck might have happened if they caught her outside out of the public eye? What if they'd felt bolder, or caught her off guard and alone?

It wasn't the first time I'd been thrown in lock-up for the night. I doubted it would be the last.

I stretched out on my back on the cot, staring up at the concrete ceiling as Aubrey drifted back into my thoughts. I heard her screaming as I took the bastard down. I felt her hands on me as she pulled me to my feet. I saw the fear in her eyes as the sirens blared, felt her fingers laced with mine as she sat by my side while they came for me. It was all blurry, but she was clear. Candace had promised to get Aubrey safely to my place and keep her there.

"I'm sorry," Aubrey had whispered in my ear as the cops pulled me out of the bar. She had nothing to be sorry about. I'd defend her with my dying breath. I should have apologized to Aubrey. If it wasn't for me and the stupid lottery...

"Where is he?"

That was Eoin's voice. I glanced up. Behind Eoin, I saw Michael and Darren stomping down the hall on the heels of a Garda named Niall. He'd been the one to process me in.

"They paid your bail," Niall said, unlocking my cell door.

"Thanks, guys," I said to my brothers as my door swung open.

I stepped forward to gain my freedom but Niall didn't move aside from the doorway. "I don't always agree, you know," he said in a soft voice. "That girl needs protecting. But try to keep your nose clean, okay? Don't want to see you back here anytime soon." He stepped back to let me walk through.

"Thank you," I said as I passed him.

"Yeah, yeah, get the fuck out."

The metal-on-metal crash of the door closing made me jump, the echo sounding in my ears like a warning clang.

My brothers dropped me off at my place.

They had all asked about Aubrey in the car. The truth was, even I didn't know. She had been shutting me out more and more since it happened. I thought that her coming to The Jar was a sign that things were turning a corner.

But what happened tonight... The hopeless look on her face as I was taken away by the Garda scared me.

I ran up the stairs two at a time towards my door, my heart banging against my ribs. I needed Aubrey, needed to feel her in my arms, to tell her that everything would be okay, to promise her it would be. I didn't know how I would keep that promise, but I would find a way.

Where there was love, there was hope.

I unlocked my door and barreled in, my eyes seeking the face of the woman I loved.

Aubrey and Candace were sitting close together on my couch, talking. As soon as they spotted me, their voices dropped. Aubrey looked at me. But the way she was looking at me was hollow, like she wasn't really here.

I glanced at Candace and found pity there, a sad smile flashed then disappeared, a brief sorry.

My guts twisted.

"I'll wait outside," Candace said to Aubrey so softly I almost missed the words. Candace refused to look at me as she walked past me.

The door closed behind me with a heavy resigned click. That sound propelled me into action.

I moved towards her. "Aubrey, I—"

"Please, don't come any closer." She stood, holding her hands out towards me like she was trying to hold me back.

I skidded to a halt several feet away from her, but it might have well been a mile.

"If you do, I might not have the strength to…" She trailed off.

The emptiness left behind in the silence began to buzz in my ears. I swallowed hard. "Strength to…?"

She shook her head, her hair falling about her face partly hiding her eyes from me. "I can't stay here anymore."

"In this apartment? Rey, you know I don't care about rent or—"

"No. I mean here…in Ireland."

Her words, so deceptively soft, yet they hit me with the force of a cannonball to the chest. I must have misheard her. Misunderstood.

"I'm moving back to the US," she whispered, drawing in a deep breath as fresh tears filled her eyes.

"*No.*" She couldn't. I waited four years for her. I couldn't lose her. Now that I'd had a taste of life with her. I needed her like I needed air.

Her eyes travelled my face, hesitating at my busted lip before scanning the rest of me. "What happened last night will keep happening," she said softly, nodding at my mouth before looking up into my eyes. "You won't always be around to protect me."

Her words felt like spears of failure. She was right. I couldn't be her bodyguard every single second of the day. She couldn't live her life in this apartment, hiding from the world.

"Even if I had the strength to ignore the public backlash," she continued, "sooner or later, someone will put two and two together. You and your brothers will be exposed."

"I don't care."

"I do. I won't risk you or your brothers." Her lips curved a tiny bit in a brave smile that didn't reach her eyes or ease the pain in her expression.

She was doing this to protect me. I was the one who was supposed to protect her. I failed.

She was right.

She had to leave.

We had to leave.

I nodded. "Okay, so we leave. We move to the States."

Her eyes widened. "W-We?"

"I'm coming with you."

She blinked at me, fresh tears brimming her lids. "Oh, Noah," she breathed the words out. She shook her head. "You have the bar here—"

"I'll sell it."

She looked stunned. "But you love The Jar."

"It's just a damn bar." I would sell it in a heartbeat if it meant not losing her. There was nowhere she would go that I wouldn't follow.

"Your brothers are here. Darren, Eoin, Michael…"

I stepped closer to her. "They are not my future; *you are*."

I felt like I was fighting the hardest battle I'd ever fought, yet it was without violence or raised voices. This exchange of words was more terrifying than anything I'd experienced before, and the stakes—losing her—were the highest I'd ever known.

"Your ma is here, and she needs you. *She needs you*," she repeated with more force.

I opened my mouth. Then shut it. What could I counter with?

That my ma didn't need me? My chest squeezed.

I cursed every God and deity under the sun for making me choose to have only *one* of the two women I loved.

"I could come back to visit…" My voice was quiet, low, almost resigned.

Aubrey shot me a small smile. "Your life is here, Noah."

"So is yours."

She shook her head.

I wanted more than anything to pull her into my arms. But I couldn't move, feeling like I was sinking into the quicksand.

"Goodbye, Noah. Thank you for everything." She tried to move past me.

The threat of her leaving was enough to unfreeze me. I stepped in front of her, blocking her path. "Don't do this."

"I'm sorry, Noah."

"We can figure something out. I'll fix this."

"You can't," she said, her voice choking up a bit like she was holding back tears.

"Do you love me?"

"It's not about love."

"It's a simple question, Rey. Do you love me?"

"With all my heart."

I grabbed her hands in mine. "Where there's love, there's hope. Remember? That's what you taught me."

Her eyes filled with tears as she tugged her hands from me and pressed them to her face. "Please, Noah. I can't—I just can't…"

"But there's hope," I begged, feeling like I was hanging desperately onto a sinking lifeboat.

There was hope.

Right?

Aubrey let out a huge sob, the sound of her pain tearing my heart into pieces. She pushed past me and flung open the door.

I couldn't move to stop her.

The love of my life just walked—ran—out of my life.

Aubrey

On the sidewalk, I collapsed into Candace's arms. She began to speak quietly to me in Portuguese, the words comforting even though I had no idea what she was saying.

He'd come out after me, wouldn't he?

I mean, I know I ran out, but that was because I had no choice. Our situation was hopeless.

Right?

"*Where there is love, there's hope.*" Noah's voice echoed in my head.

But the door didn't open. He didn't come after me.

Candace slipped an arm under my shoulder and guided me to her car, my knees trembling, threatening to give out. A burning ache crept up my chest and settled into the back of my throat.

In the car, Candace paused, her hands on the steering wheel. "Amiga, are you sure you're doing the right thing?"

No one had figured out I was hiding out here. There were no microphones shoved in my face, no one screaming personal questions at me or banging on the car windows.

The vultures hadn't found out…yet.

But they would. I had to leave to protect the man I loved. It was the right thing to do. Even if it meant that Noah would hate me forever.

I nodded. I was doing the right thing. I *was* doing the right thing. I just had to say it over and over again until I believed it. Even if it felt like I couldn't breathe around the words.

As Candace pulled the car away from the curb, I lifted my head to Noah's apartment. I don't know what I was expecting. Hoping. Maybe to see his face one last time, watching me from the window.

His blank windows stared back at me, curtains drawn.

Silent and devoid of hope.

Noah

Eoin was the last of my brothers to show up at my apartment, pink-faced and dripping sweat. I stared at him as he stood outside my door. There was already a small lake collecting at his sneakers.

"What?" he asked.

I raised an eyebrow at him.

"I was at the gym."

The other eyebrow went up.

"You said it was an emergency," Eoin said with a huff.

I stepped aside to let him in. "Fine. Come in, just…don't sit on anything. Or touch anything. Or drip on—"

"Yeah alright, asshole," he grumbled, making a point to brush past me with his shoulder, wiping sweat off onto me.

"Jaysus, boy," Darren piped up from my couch, "did you forget to dry off after your shower?"

"You know," Michael said, "there is this thing called a towel."

"Fuck all of you. I'm going back to the gym." Eoin turned on his heel.

"Stay. Please. I need your help."

My words stopped him dead in his tracks.

I looked across at the faces of all my brothers. "All of you." I closed the front door and turned to face my brothers again.

Darren and Michael were sitting on my couch.

Eoin was standing at their side.

These three men would walk into hell beside me. And I for them. For the first time since Aubrey walked out of my life, I felt hope. "She's leaving," I said in the suddenly quiet room. I didn't even have to say who *she* was. They knew. "She broke up with me and is moving back to the States. Forever." There it was. The truth hung out to dry between us.

For a second, they all just stared at me, unmoving.

"She can't," Eoin cried. "But you and she…"

"Can you blame her for leaving?" I replied. "With everything that has happened."

"You could go with her," Michael said quietly. "Ma would understand."

I shook my head. "She doesn't want me to."

"You can't give her up without a fight," Darren said.

Both Eoin and Michael agreed with a murmur and nod of their heads.

"I'm not planning to. That's why I called a meeting. I need a plan. To fix this. To get her back. Please. *Help me.*"

Aubrey

It had been two days since I split up with Noah. I could hardly find the energy to get out of bed. Out of bed being a cute term when I really meant off Candace's couch. Candace had been kind enough to let me stay with her for the time being until I could book my flight back to Austin.

My suitcases were packed already, crammed into a corner of her living room, ready to be shipped off with me to a home that didn't feel like home anymore.

I'd given notice to my landlord. Candace and another girl from the bar had been kind enough to go back to my place and pack everything up for me. When they'd gotten back, Candace had confided in me that the media was still camped out there. It made me sick to think they were practically living outside my old apartment waiting to tear me up.

I had to leave.

I sat on the couch, my laptop in my lap, staring at the flight booking web page. I had to leave. I couldn't keep living like this, cooped up in someone else's house, unable to even leave for fear of being spotted. I couldn't keep living out of suitcases and waiting for the inevitable to happen. Eventually, someone would figure out where I was. Candace didn't deserve for me to mess up her life too.

I needed to book my flight. I needed to bite the bullet and get it done. My cursor hovered over the confirm button. Noah's face sprang into mind, his voice in my ear.

"Don't do this."

"I'm sorry, Noah."

I closed my laptop and slipped it back on the coffee table before curling myself into a ball. Tomorrow, I'd book the flight and leave this life behind forever. Tomorrow, it would be easier.

"We can figure something out. I'll fix this."

"You can't."

Tears stung in my eyes, blurring my vision, as agony rippled through my chest. I sucked in a deep breath through my nose and let it out slowly. Would this pain ever lessen?

"Do you love me?"

"It's not about love."

"It's a simple question, Rey. Do you love me?"

"With all my heart."

"Where there's love, there's hope. Remember? That's what you taught me."

They said that time heals all wounds. So why did my pain grow as the minutes ticked by?

Noah

My pulse was thundering in my ears. It might work. It had to work.

It was a good idea, one that took all our brainpower and days of talking and thinking and strategizing to reach.

We were back at my place, my brothers and me. We all knew the parts we had to play. Eoin and Michael were making calls, pulling all the strings that they had access to. Darren, on his laptop, was typing away like mad, his expression taut like he knew exactly what was riding on him.

A calling tone sounded in my ear. *Come on, pick up.*

"Noah," Danny said when he answered. "Man, I'm sorry for what the media is doing to Aubrey. I wanted to call, but I figured you needed space and time."

"Thank you," I said, meaning it.

"How is she coping?"

"Not good, Danny. Not fucking good. I need your help again."

"Anything."

I took a moment to thank my lucky stars for people like this in my life, the ones who backed me without hesitation, without question, and without expecting anything in return. *These* were my people. The ones who mattered, anyway.

I let him in on the plan and he agreed, promising to make calls himself and rope some other people into it too, before we said our goodbyes.

I had another call to make. One I felt less sure of. This was the tricky one, the one that could fall apart or go wrong very quickly. I had to put aside my feelings for the man to ask him for a favor—not my favorite spot to be put in. But it would be worth it. All of it was worth it if I could get this to work.

I dialed the number and only had to wait half a ring for a response.

"Jason Reilly speaking." He sounded a bit preoccupied...until I spoke.

"It's Noah O'Sullivan. From the fundraiser."

"Who?"

"Aubrey Campbell's boyfriend," I lied just a little.

Silence.

Then a cautious, "What can I do for you?"

"I'd like to give you an exclusive scoop about Aubrey. But there's a catch," I said.

There was a shorter pause this time.

"I'm listening," he said.

Aubrey

Knock, knock.

Oh God. They'd finally found me.

I stared at Candace's apartment front door, imagining a horde of reporters on the other side.

Candace and her housemates weren't home. I was here alone. I couldn't send them to deal with whoever was knocking.

Maybe they'd go away.

The door banged again.

Fuck.

I slipped off the couch and crept to the front door in my socks. Placed my eye at the peephole, my breath stuck in my lungs.

Noah's face stared back at me.

My heart squeezed painfully. I snatched my eye off the peephole and leaned my back against the door. What was he doing here?

My mouth went dry, my heart thundering in my chest. I couldn't open the door to him. If I did, I'd give in. I hadn't even worked up the strength to book my tickets. I'd have no chance of convincing him that I didn't want to be with him if I opened that door.

"Aubrey?" His beautiful deep voice came muffled through the wood panel. "I know you're there."

I let out an *eep* and slapped my hand over my mouth.

"Please open the door."

I wanted to. So badly. But I was terrified to. I wasn't strong enough to walk away from Noah again. Doing it the first time almost killed me.

"I just want to talk. To say goodbye, if you're set on leaving."

My heart cracked. How could I deny him—deny either of us—this final farewell? He had been so much a part of my life these last four years. He'd continue to be part of me forever.

Maybe saying goodbye to Noah would give me the strength to close this chapter of my life.

With shaking hands, I unlocked the door and opened it.

Noah was as gorgeous as ever, not just through my eyes, but through my heart. Even with the dark circles under his eyes, the worried press to his lips, the hollowness to his cheeks. I wanted to pull him into my arms, to kiss his eyelids. To rest my head on his chest and listen to him breathing.

I still loved him so much. Opening the door was a mistake.

"Hey," he said, that single word so full of longing, his eyes drinking me in.

"Hey," I breathed, my hand dropping from the door. There was no way I could shut the door in his face.

No way.

"This might be too much for me to ask of you but…"

Anything. Noah, you know you can ask me for anything.

"Will you come with me one last time before you leave Ireland?"

Anywhere. I'd go anywhere with him. I wanted to step into his arms, have him wrap me up and take me away. Wherever he wanted to go.

I swallowed, trying to keep myself from leaping at him to close the distance. "I don't know, Noah."

"Please. I want to show you something." The look on his face was filled with desperate longing.

I could barely stand to look at him. "Okay," dropped from my lips.

His face broke into a look of relief.

I wondered if I was going to regret this decision. Did I just make it impossible to say goodbye to him?

"Where are you taking me?" I asked, not moving.

He offered me his hand. "Do you trust me?"

Damn him. I glanced down at his muscular arm stretching across the canyon between us, to his strong hand. Of course I trusted him.

I reached for him, my hand sliding into his and our fingers lacing. It felt like a homecoming. Like two puzzle pieces clicking together. *Stupid, Aubrey. How will you ever let go of him now?*

"And you can't see anything?" Noah asked, adjusting the blindfold on my eyes.

"I can't see anything," I assured him.

I'd be lying if I said I wasn't a tiny bit nervous about this whole elaborate set-up. In the car, Noah had blindfolded me before pulling the seatbelt across and clicking it into place. He'd driven us in silence to here, wherever here was.

Noah got out of the car and opened the passenger door for me, helping me out.

A moment later Noah's hand slipped around my shoulder. He held me close to him as we walked across a hard surface.

"Where are we?"

"A few more minutes. I promise." His voice vibrated with energy.

I heard a door swing open and Noah led me through it.

The scent of cut grass hit me along with a fresh breeze. Light came through the blindfold. The flat surface turned to grass under my feet. I could hear a murmur around us, but I couldn't figure out where we were or what was happening.

"Okay, stop right here," Noah said.

Goosebumps raced up and down my arms as he pulled the blindfold off my head. I blinked as my eyes adjusted.

We were standing on the field of Aviva Stadium. Noah had taken me to the US versus Ireland rugby match here last year. One that Eoin had been playing in. We'd sat up in the VIP section thanks to Eoin, and Noah had patiently explained the rules to me.

Jesus Christ. There were thousands of people here. Almost every seat was filled. Everyone held up handmade signs that read: #YesToHer.

"What's going on, Noah?"

Noah was smiling. At least that gave me comfort. He pointed to the big screen in answer.

The crowd cheered as Danny O'Donaghue came up on screen. From the background it looked like he was sitting in a sparsely furnished apartment, so this must be a recording.

His brows furrowed over his blue eyes as he spoke directly into the camera. "Men have been allowed their sexual desires. After all, boys will be boys, right?" Danny's lip curled. "Today, women are *told* they are equal, but let's be honest…that is still a fucking lie. Because the four men that Aubrey had a *consensual, adult* connection with are heroes. While she is just a slut."

The crowd shouted and booed this statement.

"Change starts by being conscious of the problem. By choosing *not* to accept it. To refuse to join in with the ones bleating like a bunch of mindless sheep. And by standing up for the thing you believe in. By spreading a new message. Change starts with Aubrey." He paused as if for effect and the crowd went nearly silent. "My name is Danny O'Donaghue. And I'm saying yes to *her* pleasure, too."

The stadium roared as they lifted and shook their signs.

I just stared around me, unable to believe what I was seeing, hearing.

Gone were the disgusted looks, the jokes at my expense. In its place were smiles, encouragement.

I never knew I had such support. It seemed that the critics with their judgments were screaming louder than the quiet voices of agreement. Except for today.

Today, these quiet voices weren't being quiet anymore.

I turned to the man I knew had orchestrated this. To thank him. "Noah…"

But he wasn't done yet. He turned me gently and pointed back up to the screen. Danny's face faded off screen.

I watched, my mouth hanging open, as the screen began to cut to famous faces I recognized—musicians, actors, actresses—all voicing their support. All holding signs with #YesToHer.

Holy shit.

"You did this," I choked out to Noah.

"We did."

We?

He turned me to face the players' section behind us. There in the box closest to the field were Candace, Eoin, Michael and Darren. And a face I didn't expect to see: Mrs. O'Sullivan.

She shook her #YesToHer sign as our gazes locked.

I began to choke on my relief, on the love I felt vibrating through this stadium. Like a lotus, something beautiful had grown out of mud. Gathering speed and volume, the sky filled with the chant of "yes to her, yes to her."

Ireland believed in me. Supported me.

They believed in my right to enjoy the consensual, intimate night of passion that I'd had. They believed that no one had the right to shame me or judge me for it. They believed that a woman should desire without fear.

I began to cry. Ugly cry. Tears streaming down my face, between my fingers. My chest constricting so hard that it hurt.

Noah pulled me into his arms and held me tight, murmuring words over the deafening sound of the crowd. "You don't have to leave. You don't have to hide," he said, just for me. "I know there will still be people here that don't agree, but look at how many do. They've just found a voice. And they are louder than the hate. Because of you."

We were surrounded by strangers and family alike, but I'd never felt so close to him, like we were the only two people on the planet.

I couldn't believe he'd done this. All of this. It hardly seemed possible. A week ago, I was sure I couldn't love him more. But he'd proven me wrong.

"I'm sorry," he said, pulling back, his blue eyes darting back and forth between mine. "I didn't do it right the first time."

Didn't do what right?

Noah took both my hands in his.

As he lowered to one knee, my heart began to race in my chest, and every drop of saliva in my mouth dried up.

He pulled out a little black box from his pocket.

Somewhere in my brain, a scream like a steam engine whistle began to sound. Within the box was a beautiful ring with a diamond nestled between two trinity knots.

The crowd rose up again, cheering and clapping, a thunderous roar. But all I saw, all I heard, was him. Noah. His blue eyes locked on mine.

"I don't care if we live here or the US or in a cabin in northern Iceland. *You* are my home. Marry me?" He looked so equally hopeful and terrified.

This was the man, my man, the man I loved more than anything. He'd done all of this for me.

I nodded, a *yes* bubbling out of my mouth.

The dimpled smile that he rewarded me with made my heart feel full to bursting even as my tears started up again. God, he was gorgeous. To my eyes. And to my heart.

He slipped the ring on my finger before standing up and pulling me into his arms. Our mouths met. Everything else faded away, the screams of the crowd, the cheering, the applause, it all dulled. I could see, hear and feel Noah. His lips on mine, the sweet mint taste of his kiss, the promises he was silently giving me.

We could get through anything, so long as we stood side by side. I was sure of it.

I was no longer afraid.

Let the world come at me, judge me, try to bring me down.

I'd face it all head-on because I had the ones I loved in my corner. And a cause worth fighting for.

Later, in the quiet of Noah's apartment, away from the crowds, from the crackle and roar of the wildfire we had somehow started, Noah and I stood facing each other.

No masks.

No secrets.

No goodbyes.

Our future stretched like a long road to the horizon before us. But the only thing that I focused on, was right now.

Him and me.

My breath shuddered out past my teeth as he peeled clothing off me, replacing the material with his lips. My fingers felt thick and unwieldly as I yanked at his clothes. He chuckled as he helped me, kicking off his shoes, undoing his troublesome belt, divesting himself of his jeans. Our lips—chests, skin, hands— clashing in a glorious mess. We tumbled to the bed. My legs wrapping around his waist, pulling him in close, my hips shifting, his erection sliding around between us as I tried to find where we fit best.

I was ready to beg if he pulled back, if he wanted to torture me with foreplay. God knows, four years was long enough to wait.

These last few days of separation had created a distance that only one thing could fill.

I didn't have to beg.

He tilted his hips and slid into me as naturally and easily as falling in love with him had been.

Raw pleasure and naked love crackled through my body like two electrical currents waltzing around each other. My eyes stung, emotion like fast-blooming leaves off the branches of my lungs, choking me with its violent delight.

"Noah," I gasped, trying to speak, trying to convey the wordless feelings coursing through my body. Trying to tell him that I found heaven. Trying to tell him that I was his and always would be.

His eyes, filled with more depth than the ocean, glossy as the midday surface of the sea, held my gaze. They told me, *I know. I feel it, too.*

Every thrust was a promise, every kiss smoothing away the roughness of our secrets, both his and mine.

He rolled us over until I was on top of him. I sat up, running my greedy palms over the ridges of his beautiful body, reveling in the new places he touched me from the inside.

"Fuck," shuddered from his mouth as he gazed up at me as if he was seeing the stars for the first time. "You're the most beautiful thing I've ever seen."

And I believed him.

His fingers dug into my hips as I rocked over him. Harder.

Faster. Spurred on by the look in his eyes and the growing feeling in my core.

I came hard around him, the force of it ripping apart any last shred of reservation. Any last piece of me that wasn't his.

And when I came to, I was lying on his chest, his arms around me like a shield, holding me closer than I'd ever been held.

"The first of many," he promised into my hair before he rolled me to my back.

Epilogue: Aubrey

The #YesToHer hashtag spread like wildfire, blazing everything it touched. Everybody was talking about it—men, woman, teenagers and the elderly—everyone had something to say. Surprisingly, most of it was supportive, not hateful, as if the bright lights of many voices had shunned the mean ones into silence.

A search of the hashtag on social media revealed result after result of women with similar stories, their truths, their experiences, shameful hearts getting to blood-let in the open.

There was no border around women who'd been targeted. It was everyone, no "type" or specifics. Religion didn't play into it. Class, money, where they lived; none of that mattered.

Women of all ages, sizes, colors, backgrounds, were speaking out and people finally seemed to be taking heed and listening. This gave me hope.

We were talking about it now. Acknowledging it. That's where change started.

#YesToHer no longer belonged to me. Although it started with me. It was *ours*. Together, we lifted each other.

Around me, the disapproving looks turned to smiles, nods, winks. Mostly. There were still disapproving looks, but now I was empowered to lift my chin in response.

It was a beautiful shift. One that made my heart feel full. Left me feeling connected and loved.

Some people asked for my autograph and pictures with me. Random women and men alike thanked me and some apologized. I was suddenly an "inspiration"—which I didn't agree with. I hadn't done anything. Noah was the one who did it. Noah and his brothers. And Danny, who had spearheaded his famous friends into action. And Jason, who had been the first to broadcast this new message. There were good men in the world. They'd stepped up to help me when I needed it most. I would be forever grateful.

I'd started to screen print tee shirts with the #YesToHer hashtag and sold them on a website built—and maintained— by Darren. It had grown almost overnight into a business that put me on track to earn more in a year than I had in all my life leading up to that point. It grew more and more every day.

The business had exploded so quickly, I'd been able to apply for a self-employment visa. I'd done so, just to remove any doubt about why I was marrying Noah. I loved him and I was marrying him for one reason and one reason only...I couldn't imagine life without him. He was my family, my home, my best friend. I wanted him there by my side every day for the rest of my life.

I'd moved into his apartment immediately. Why wait? We'd known each other for four years already. "World's longest foreplay," he'd joked.

With a happy sigh, I pulled my laptop onto my lap, still unable to really believe everything was going so well. It seemed like a dream; too good to be true. I found myself often having to pinch myself. I'd found my email inbox flooded with various opportunities to speak out in Ireland and throughout Europe. I was considering it. Nothing was set in stone yet.

I could feel Noah looking at me and glanced up.

He was standing in the doorway, looking as handsome as ever, in jeans and a light-blue long-sleeved pullover that brought out his eyes, his honey-wheat hair falling over his forehead.

My heart skipped in my chest. Was this beautiful man really mine?

"Are you ready?" Noah asked.

I blinked. "Is it time to go already?"

"Just about. We don't want to be late." He walked across the room to me, moved the laptop aside before pulling me to my feet and crushed me to his chest.

His scent of fresh soap and man washed over me. Feeling so very at home and loved, I let out a contented sigh. I wound my arms around his neck and he lowered his lips to mine. I clung to him, deepening the kiss, my body igniting to wildfire.

He pulled away with a groan, a smile on his lips. "If you keep doing that, we really will be late."

A short while later we pulled up before the O'Sullivan childhood home. Noah was quick to hurry around and open my door with a low bow. I giggled at his show of chivalry. From the back of the car, he grabbed the insulated bag containing the lasagna I'd baked earlier, still warm enough to make the car smell like rich beef sauce and melted cheese, and took my hand in his.

A wolf whistle cut through the still suburban air.

I grinned at Eoin over my shoulder.

Beside me, Noah growled, "We're engaged now, that shit won't fly."

"You've got food in your hand, I'm safe," Eoin said, walking right past us, up into the house carrying his own bag.

"My hands aren't full!" I called after him.

"They should be!" he shouted.

Then there was a yelp as Ma smacked him upside the head before chewing him out.

Darren and Michael laughed from the armchairs in the living room where they lounged.

"When will he learn?" Michael asked.

Darren snorted. "He won't."

"Part of my charm," Eoin said as he walked into the living room, having escaped Ma's wrath. For now.

Noah shook his head.

I giggled before heading off in search of Ma while the guys set the table like they'd done a million times before.

All the fear I'd had about it being awkward with his brothers turned out to be unfounded. No one treated me any differently, there was no mention of it, and honestly, it was like it never even happened. Strange, but I found myself feeling grateful for all of it. Without that whole mess, Noah and I might have never gotten together. Without having our limits tested, we might have never realized how strong we could be or how important we were in each other's lives.

I found Ma in the kitchen that smelled like meat and herbs from the various dishes that were reheating in the oven.

Mrs. O'Sullivan looked up from the huge salad bowl she was throwing chopped cherry tomatoes into and rewarded me with a brilliant smile. "Hello, love."

"Miriam," I said, giving her a quick hug, "you didn't have to make anything." Even though she was doing better than ever, we still all insisted that she didn't cook for Sunday lunches.

Mrs. O'Sullivan let out a snort. "You know these boys' idea of vegetable is mashed potatoes. *Someone* had to add some greenery to the table."

I chuckled. "Need a hand?"

"If you could sort out a few avocados for me, that'd be grand."

I spotted the avocados in the fruit basket and went in search of a chopping board and a knife.

"Noah tells me your business is doing so well."

I flushed. "It is."

"He says you're still pulling shifts at The Jar though."

"I love that bar," I admitted, carefully running a knife around the first avocado. "It never feels like work."

I looked up to find Mrs. O'Sullivan beaming at me. She pulled me into her arms. "I'm so proud of you," she said, clinging tightly to me. "Couldn't have asked for a better daughter."

I hugged her back, feeling so loved, my heart was near bursting. I had joined the O'Sullivans and felt like the luckiest girl alive. I had brothers who cared about me, a mother who accepted me for who I was, and a tight-knit family I could count on for anything.

I wanted to tell her how much her support meant to me, how much of a difference it made, but I couldn't get the words out. I couldn't even tell her how much I loved her because of the painful lump in my throat. I had a feeling she knew, though. Ma always seemed to know.

"You know," she said, pulling back once more with a wicked gleam in her eyes. "I was a wild child once." She winked at me. "How do you think I ended up with so many sons, after all?"

"Table's all set." Noah appeared at the kitchen door. He looked between his ma and me. "What are you guys talking about?"

"Nothing!" Ma and I said at the same time. Ma winked at me and we both burst out laughing.

"I feel like I missed something," Noah said, frowning.

"Just women talking, dear," Ma said, giving me a knowing smile. "Just women talking."

Later that evening, Noah and I were the only ones left closing at the end of the shift at The Jar. Like it always had been.

A thrill ran down my spine as Noah placed a hand on my lower back. I'd expected the sheer excitement I felt in his presence to ease up a little bit, but over the course of the year, it had only seemed to grow stronger. I glanced up at him with a smile as he dropped a kiss on the tip of my nose and another to my lips. He pulled away with a little noise of pleasure before coming right back in again and giving me another kiss like he couldn't get enough.

"Why don't you take a break," he said gently. "I'll sort the rest."

"Are you sure?"

He nodded. "You look wiped out."

I nodded. I was feeling a bit tired on my feet. I slid onto a stool as he got behind the bar and planted his hands shoulder-width apart. The move flexed his arms, and I found myself staring even as my mouth started watering. He looked good enough to eat.

His blue eyes locked on mine, full of fun and love. "What can I getcha, *Mrs.* O'Sullivan?" he asked.

I giggled. I still felt a thrill at hearing my new surname.

I planted my elbows on the bar and stared up at him through my lashes. "Just you, barkeep."

"You don't want a Guinness?" he asked.

I shook my head.

"How about a cider? Orchard Thieves?"

I slid off the bar, walking around it and into his arms. He held me close and I let this sense of peace wash over me. Things would change. But for now, I would hold onto what we were.

"No drinks for me," I said softly.

"Are you okay?" he asked, his eyebrows coming together. This man had an uncanny knack for knowing when something was on my mind or when I simply wasn't feeling well. Obviously, he was picking up on that right then.

I nodded, a grin escaping me. I wiggled around in his arms so my back was to his front. I placed my hands over his currently holding my hips. I slid both our hands around me and over my belly. Already I could feel the gentle swell there. I knew he could feel it too, from his sharp intake of breath.

He turned me to face him, hope and awe shining in his eyes. "Really? You're…?"

I couldn't contain the happiness anymore, my little secret beaming from my face. I nodded. "We've just won the best lottery…ever."

The End

Dear Readers

Thank you for reading *The Irish Lottery*. What I love about writing romance is that we women get our desires, wants and needs placed front and center.
Without apology.
Without shame.
Bit by bit we create a world where our pleasure and our needs are as important as his.
#YesToHer
#YesToYou

Stay sexy,
xoxo Sienna

www.siennablake.com
www.facebook.com/SiennaBlakeAuthor
www.instagram.com/SiennaBlakeAuthor

PS. Remember those three Irish billionaires who wanted the waitresses name? That sexy story coming soon…

Please post a review

Did you enjoy *The Irish Lottery?*
Please consider leaving a review! Just one sentence. One word.
An emoji!

It really helps other readers to decide whether my books are for them. And the number of reviews I get is super important.

Thank you!

Join my Newsletter

Never miss a new release again!

No spam. No junky emails. Ever.

www.siennablake.com

Join my Reader Group

You'll get access to Advanced Review Copies of my books, exclusive giveaways, sneak peeks into what's coming up next, and get to vote on covers, titles and blurbs.

http://bit.ly/SiennasDarkAngels

Join my Bloggers List

If you're a Blogger, please sign up to my Bloggers List for ARC opportunity alerts in your inbox.

http://bit.ly/SiennaVIPBloggers

Blogs will be verified.

Professor's Kiss

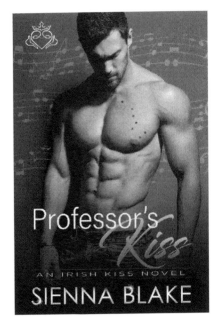

Danny O'Donaghue.

Indie rock god.

Lady killer.

The devil with midnight hair and blue-flame eyes.

After six years I thought the pain of what he'd done to me had faded.

Guess not.

Because I'm standing in this crowded lecture hall of the most prestigious music school in Ireland, staring at the person who healed me when I was broken. Right before he shattered me beyond repair.

And I still feel *everything*.

My ex-best friend.

My first love.

My tormentor.

…is now my *professor*.

Out now

Three Irish Brothers

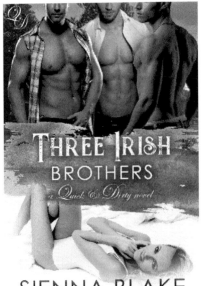

I used to think I was one of the lucky ones.

But at twenty-six, I've left my "perfect" life in New York behind and ended up in Ireland.

When my car hits a ditch I'm rescued by the three sexiest men I've ever seen.

The three Irish O'Callaghan brothers.

Broad shoulders, strong arms, accents that make me wet just to hear them.

Killian, the bossy one.

Fionn, the cheeky one.

And Aiden, the silent one with a secret.

They all want me.

I want them. All of them.

I have to choose...right? Or will I be the thing that tears this family apart.

Warning: This is a sexy yet emotional reverse-harem romance, a full-length, standalone novel at 50k words. Three sexy Irish brothers who want nothing more than to please their special woman. All at the same time.

Sienna's Quick & Dirty series consists of standalone novels which are hotter, dirtier and quicker than her other novels.

Books by Sienna Blake

Irish Kiss (Standalone Series)
Irish Kiss
Professor's Kiss
Fighter's Kiss ~ *coming soon*
The Irish Lottery

Quick & Dirty (Standalone Series)
Three Irish Brothers
My Irish Kings
Royally Screwed

A Good Wife (Standalone Series)
Beautiful Revenge
Mr. Blackwell's Bride

Bound Duet
Bound by Lies (#1)
Bound Forever (#2)

Dark Romeo Trilogy
Love Sprung From Hate (#1)
The Scent of Roses (#2)
Hanging in the Stars (#3)

Paper Dolls

About Sienna

Sienna Blake is a dirty girl, a wordspinner of smexy love stories and an Amazon Top 20 & USA Today Bestselling Author.

She's an Australian living in Dublin, Ireland, where she enjoys reading, exploring this gorgeous country and adding to her personal harem of Irish hotties ;)

Printed in Great Britain
by Amazon

43931937R00225